Praise for *The Continuum*

"Nikel's inventive spin on time travel and eye for sumptuous detail make her writing a treat to read."

—Publishers Weekly

"*The Continuum* packs a staggering amount of well drawn world-building into a short space, making for enough time travel adventure to launch a series...full of heart, humor, and thrilling action and adventure scenes that make for a fun, fast read."

—*Foreword Reviews*

"Nikel's time travel narrative is brisk and energetic, with a relatively straightforward and action oriented plot...those interested in a light and enjoyable SF read in the style of popular time-travel tropes such as *Doctor Who* should give it a look."

—*IndiePicks Magazine*

"Fans of Jules Verne, *Dr. Who* and *Quantum Leap* (minus the body jumping) should settle in for a time traveling puzzle that keeps our heroine on her toes."

—Tangent Online

"Nikel is a solid writer with vivid description, an imaginative future, and a command of accurate historical speech."

—Unreliable Narrators

The Continuum

A Place in Time Novella

(Book #1)

Wendy Nikel

World Weaver Press

THE CONTINUUM

Wendy Nikel
Copyright © 2018 Wendy Nikel.

Published by World Weaver Press, LLC
Albuquerque, NM
www.WorldWeaverPress.com
Editor: Rhonda Parrish

Cover layout and design by Sarena Ulibarri.
Cover images used under license from Shutterstock.com.

First edition: January 2018
ISBN-13: 978-0998702223

Also available as an ebook

THE CONTINUUM

THE PLACE IN TIME TRAVEL AGENCY'S TEN ESSENTIAL RULES OF TIME TRAVEL

1. Travelers must return to their original era as scheduled.

2. Travelers are prohibited from Jumping to any time they have already experienced.

3. Travel dates must be prior to the traveler's birth.

4. Travel within the Black Dates is prohibited.*

5. Only pre-approved objects may be taken into the past.

6. Travelers are prohibited from disclosing information about PITTA or its excursions.

7. Travelers are prohibited from disclosing any foreknowledge to people of the past.

8. Travelers must avoid all unnecessary fraternization with people of past eras.

9. Extractions must occur in secure, unobservable locations.

10. After Extraction, clients must immediately return their Wormhole Devices to PITTA headquarters.

*for complete list of Black Dates, see PITTA handbook Appendix B

THE PAST

CHAPTER ONE: APRIL 9, 1912

The imposing Romanesque architecture reminds me of a fairy-tale castle, with its arched windows, parapets, and rough-faced stone. Vines crawl up a corner tower, and the scents of freesia and lilac waft through the air. As I climb the steps, I search for signs of life but see none aside from the pair of sparrows hopping boldly across a stone lion's nose.

I rap on a door knocker, and my gaze follows the flow of etched swirls and vines that encircle the doorway and meet at the top with an elaborate capstone of a face. It glares down at me as if it knows I don't belong here.

The door shudders and the handle rattles so violently that when it creaks open I'm startled by the tiny, narrow-faced woman peering out from behind it.

"May I help you, miss?"

It's show time.

I flash my warmest smile and carefully consider my accent before speaking. "I wish to speak with Miss van Grete."

It isn't her real name, of course. Not that anyone in 1912 would recognize the twenty-something pop star, but one can never be too careful when touring the past.

"Who's calling?" the maid asks.

"My name is Elise Morley. Marie and I knew one another in New York, and when I read of her engagement in the paper this morning, I simply had to stop by and congratulate her personally. Is she home?"

I pull the clipping from today's *Daily Telegraph* from between the pages of my notebook. It's proof of the client's infractions, starting with the fact that she's still here when she ought to have already returned from her little vacation. When I Jumped back to 1912 New York to Retrieve her, I discovered she'd relocated to London, where she'd somehow convinced an influential businessman that she was his long-lost niece. What's worse, she also won the heart of a local gentleman, known for his scientific genius and his family's sizeable fortune.

Her blatant disregard for the Rules is the worst I've ever seen.

The maid nudges the door open further, but her slight frame still blocks my view. "Very sorry, miss. She left with her fiancé yesterday. He's arranged a trip for the two of them as a surprise engagement gift."

A new hire, then, obviously. Any seasoned domestic servant would know better than to gossip with her employers' callers.

"Will they return soon?"

"Afraid not. They're bound for America, so he might ask her father for her hand in marriage face to face."

Curious, considering her father hasn't been born yet.

"Of course! How very proper. I do hate that I missed an opportunity to see her, though." *Again*, I silently fume. "When do they depart?"

I check my PITTA-issued watch, which displays not only the current time and date, but also the time and date in my own present. April 9. I'm running out of time.

"Noon tomorrow. Out of Southampton." She beams at me and leans in closer, as if imparting a great secret. "They will be crossing on the *Titanic*!"

Fortunately, she obviously misreads my horrified expression for surprise and continues. "I've been reading about it in the papers for weeks and would never have expected Miss Marie would have the luck of being one of its first passengers. Oh, not that the master couldn't afford the tickets himself."

"Of course." I'm only half-listening. Dr. Wells is not going to be happy about this.

"But he is always too busy to travel, and Miss Marie will be delighted at all of the wonderful amenities. And the company they shall keep!"

I nod absentmindedly as she rattles off the names and occupations of all the Duff-Gordons and Ismays and Rothschilds and Strauses and Hayses who will be aboard. The names clatter around in my brain, and I try to recall which of them will survive.

"Were they going directly to Southampton from here?"

"Oh, yes." Her head bobbles up and down. "They booked rooms at the South Western Hotel."

"Thank you so much for your help. If you'll excuse me, I believe I shall see what trains are running to Southampton. Perhaps I may even catch a glimpse of this famous *Titanic* myself."

CHAPTER TWO: APRIL 10, 1912

The South Western Hotel's lobby is vast and luxurious, appropriate lodging for the first-class passengers awaiting their voyage. Chandeliers hang from coffered ceilings, and above each door, half-moon scenes of Greek mythology give the room a classical air. The excitement of the *Titanic*'s departure tingles through the groups of waiting travelers, manifesting itself in hushed whispers and nervous laughter, as porters scramble around them.

I check my watch. 11:00 A.M. on April 10, 1912. The wrongness of my presence here weighs on me. It's a Black Date, one of the periods of time that Dr. Wells has deemed too dangerous or too pivotal in history to risk traveling. Linchpins, one might say. I'm stuck with two terrible options, but in this case, leaving Marie van Grete here alone seems the more dangerous choice.

"Pardon me?" I lean against the front desk's polished surface.

"How may I help you?" Exhaustion overshadows the clerk's face, though he tries admirably to hide it.

"A friend of mine has a room here, and I wondered—"

"Sorry, miss," he says, as if sensing my intentions. "I'm not permitted to give out room numbers."

"Of course not! I only wish to know if Miss van Grete has

departed for the docks yet." I bat my eyelashes at him.

He hesitates but turns to his records. "She has not yet turned in her key."

"Oh, thank goodness! You've been ever so helpful!" I beam at him. I'm rewarded with a hint of a smile as he returns to his work.

I stand guard over the lobby, my toes tapping impatiently against the sea-green rug. Finally, she appears, gliding through the doorway on a gentleman's arm as if walking a red carpet. She whispers to him, and he laughs in response.

Her carelessness unsettles me. Most runaway clients would be watching over their shoulder, suspicious that any stranger might be the Retrieval Specialist sent to apprehend them. She has to know we'll be coming; it's in the contract.

I follow them out the door, strategizing how to get her alone, even for a moment, so I can complete the Extraction without breaking yet another Rule. Southampton's bustling Canute Road is hardly a "secure, private location."

Her companion's top hat bobs through the crowd, making it easy to keep them in sight. Finally, an opportunity arises. Just before the harbor comes into view, a second man joins them, slapping Marie's fiancé on the back so forcefully he nearly drops the black, leather-bound journal he's carrying. The gentlemen laugh and shake hands, but their animated conversation isn't loud enough to hear over the crowd.

A small boy of about eight years old rushes by. I grab his shoulder.

"Hey! Lemme go!" He glares up at me through tangled blonde curls, and I know instantly that he'll fit the task perfectly.

"See that woman over there?" I point to Marie.

He nods, lips still clamped shut.

I quickly count out a few coins into my palm, careful to keep one eye on Marie and her companions. "I'll give you three-halfpence to knap that woman's handbag." The boy gawks at me.

"Are you off your onion?" He pulls away, but his gaze never leaves the coins. "You must think me a juggins, askin' me to flimp that haybag, what with 'er flash toff right there, an' all the crushers out today!"

"Oh, tosh! A fine tooler like yourself; you'd do it even without my encouragement!"

"Fo' no less than a sprat."

"Done." I hand him the coins. He shoots me one final squinty-eyed look before running off and nearly knocks Marie over before disappearing into the crowd.

"Allen! That boy stole my purse!" Marie points in the direction where he'd disappeared. I wait, muscles tensed.

A frown wrinkles the gentleman's brow, and he signals for his porter. He lowers his head to speak briskly and watches with grim resolve as the hired man darts off toward the nearest cluster of policemen. I curse under my breath. Of *course* the gentleman would delegate the work to the lower classes. He gives Marie a pat on the arm, reassures her in hushed tones, and leads her toward the White Star Dock's Berth 44.

As I round the corner, there it is. The enormous mass of steel and machinery looks so noble, so deceptively steadfast. The smokestacks form a perfect line, like four giant tin soldiers standing guard, and flags flutter up and down its length, lending a festive air.

My eyes are drawn to the first-class promenade deck and to the skeletal davits emerging from it, reaching out over the edge. I squint, trying to count each one and imagining the lifeboats—far too few—that will be lowered from them in a mere matter of days. I have to Retrieve Marie. Now.

A crowd of thousands has converged on the dock, and I wedge myself between two men in bowler hats to keep Marie in my line of sight. The crowd threatens to smother me as it surges forward toward the gangways where the passengers are boarding the ship.

"Oh! Allen," Marie says, "I had a letter for Aunt Clara in my bag. I do hope the police find it before we set sail. Perhaps you could persuade the captain to send a telegram for me while on board? Aunt Clara would be thrilled to receive a message from the middle of the ocean. That would more than compensate for the loss of the letter."

"Anything for you, Mademoiselle." Allen presses her fingers to his lips. He gestures to their party's third member, a man with sharp features similar to his own. "Henry met Captain Smith at a party last spring; perhaps he can arrange an introduction."

"I found the captain to be a fine gentleman." Henry takes off his spectacles and shines them on a handkerchief. "His retirement will be quite the loss for the White Star Line."

"Always the pessimist," Allen chides.

Henry frowns, his forehead wrinkling beneath his black top hat. Strangely, it seems to me his scowl is directed more at Marie than Allen, but she's too busy tugging on her beloved's arm to notice.

"Allen, look! It's Ida Straus!" She unhooks her arm from his and melts into the mass of people. Henry, meanwhile, has drawn Allen's attention away with a question about the quantities of coal needed for the voyage. This may be my best chance.

"Miss van Grete?" I say softly, taking hold of her arm. The men's deep voices resonate through the crowd, and Marie glances over her shoulder at them before giving me a puzzled look.

"Do I know you?"

"I work for a travel agency in New York. You are a client of ours."

Normally at this point, a wayward traveler's fight or flight defense mechanisms kick in. I tense, ready to block her escape, but she simply blinks at me.

Something's not right.

"Truly? Oh, you must have a fabulous memory for faces." She smiles warmly. "I am sorry to admit that I cannot recall much about my previous voyage at all!"

"Here." I pull one of the orbs out of my handbag: a Wormhole Device. Its surface is charcoal black, sleek, nearly liquid in appearance, except for one tiny circle indentation.

"What—?" She reaches for it, but the crowd surges forward, jostling us. Allen turns, searching for her.

"Darling, you wandered off. We must be more careful; I'd hate to lose you in this crowd." He tucks his journal under his arm and reaches for her. She allows him to steer her gently back toward the line. His eyes linger on me, and I hurriedly tuck the device into my handbag. His mouth tightens under his sleek black mustache. How much did he see?

"Of course, Allen." Marie nods a parting to me and, arm in arm, they weave their way back to Henry. I watch, powerless, as they climb the steps of the gangway.

I can't let her board that ship. I push through the crowd as the trio approaches the upper gangplank that extends from the shore to the ship. Allen releases Marie's arm so they can climb single-file onto the steel structure. His attention is on his conversation with Henry as they step out over the water. I pick up my skirts to run.

"Oh, my!" A gray-haired woman gasps as I push past her. The pug curled in her arms yaps and strains toward me. So much for blending in.

My mind races. I try to put together a scenario where I *don't* end up breaking yet another Rule. It's too late, I realize with a sinking feeling. I should've been more aggressive. I should've called for backup. I should've acted sooner.

I've nearly reached them as Henry disappears into the ship. Allen fumbles in his waistcoat pocket for their boarding passes. They're mere steps from the ship.

Disregarding her alarmed gasp, I grab Marie's arm. In one swift motion, I pull the Wormhole from my bag and thrust it into her palm. She looks at it, then up at me with eyes wide and pink lips parted in surprise. With a reassuring nod, I press her thumb down on the button.

In a flash of light, she disappears.

Allen drops his journal, its thump on the gangplank barely audible over the crowd's chatter. A glimmer of light reflects off the silver compass rose embossed on its cover. A quick look over my shoulder assures me that the density and excitement of the crowd has worked to my advantage; no one else seems to have noticed a woman blink out of existence. Except Allen.

He lunges, eyes full of fury, and I jam my thumb down on the second orb's button.

My world bursts into light of saturated color as I'm Extracted—yanked back to the present like the pull of a bungee cord.

I squeeze my eyes shut, trying not to worry about the spectacle on the gangplank. Even if people in the crowd notice, their minds will fabricate a more plausible explanation for the event.

I hope.

CHAPTER THREE: APRIL 11, 1912

Allen

Allen Theodore Mansfield Reeves III spent the first day at sea locked in his stateroom in utter despair, and his brother—never known for being particularly patient—could no longer tolerate such nonsense.

Henry stepped stiffly into his brother's stateroom and balked. His younger sibling lay on the bed, the linens tumbling over him onto the floor. One arm hung over the side, his hand clutching a glass of wine. Some of the spirits seemed to have missed the glass and had seeped into the cream-colored rug, leaving a dark red stain. Nearby sat a fine china platter with the White Star Line logo, bearing a half-eaten pastry from the morning's breakfast menu.

"Get up. Now." Henry tugged the linens onto the floor, leaving his brother—still clad in the shirt and undergarments of the previous day's traveling suit—lying in an undignified mess. Henry snatched up a hand mirror from Marie's open valise on the table and held it in front of his brother's face. "Look at yourself. You're a disgrace."

Allen grumbled, refusing to make eye contact with his own haggard, red-eyed reflection. "I'd rather not discuss it."

Henry pulled up a chair to face him. "You may not want to hear it, but there are things about your beloved which you have been too blinded by your affection to notice."

"You're just bitter that things aren't as they were before," Allen said, his voice hoarse with disuse.

"How true! So you admit that you've changed in the last month? How many times have I been forced to find another, less worthy companion to accompany me to the card tables or riding stables or billiard parlors while you strolled along the beach or wandered the estate gardens with Miss Marie van Grete? You have changed, and I'm tired of being second to your latest obsession.

"Allen, that day you met her at my office, you knew that Miss van Grete was a patient of mine, correct? What did she tell you of her ailment?"

Allen's jaw tensed. He looked away but, after a moment, answered. "We discussed it at length. She has certain gaps in her memory, but she told me the two of you were making progress during her sessions."

"How much did she tell you about her parents?" Henry asked. "Anything at all, aside from their names and occupations?"

Allen continued to glare, stone-faced and silent, and Henry took that as answer enough.

"That's because she *could* not. My correspondents in New York have never even *heard* of the van Gretes. She's a liar. She has no fortune, no connections, no inheritance, nothing!" He slid his pipe from his jacket and lit it. Smoke rose from his mouth as he leaned back to observe his younger sibling.

"And her aunt?"

"Duped like the rest of us." Henry shrugged. "Dear Aunt Clara did indeed have a younger sister who ran off to America with the gardener years ago, but according to my sources, that sister died soon afterward of diphtheria, thus explaining her lack of recent communication."

"You're lying. You'd have told me sooner."

"Sooner? You've known the girl a *month*! No one expected you to propose to her so quickly, and once the deed was done…well, I assumed that upon our arrival, the truth would come out. You'd call off the engagement, and I would not have to be cast as the villain in this sordid tale. In fact, I was looking forward to being the heroic source of comfort and strength on your journey back to England. Why do you think I insisted on joining you? I had to ensure you didn't do anything drastic once you found out."

Allen's eyes narrowed. "It doesn't matter. I love her, even if she doesn't have a shilling to her name. She must have had a good reason for her deception, and I won't allow you to slander her."

"And if she is not merely a liar, but clinically insane?" Henry raised one eyebrow.

"I will not have you telling lies about her," Allen said, pushing himself upright.

"Oh, it is no lie. Miss van Grete suffered from strange dreams and visions which she believed were premonitions of the future." Henry paused to let the words sink in. "Her dreams caused extreme paranoia, as well as stomachaches and headaches brought on by her anxiety. She believed she'd been hypnotized, that someone had purposely caused her to forget her past, and she didn't know why."

"Why didn't she tell me?"

Henry shrugged. "She thought she was protecting you. According to her, there were people coming to get her…to 'retrieve' her. She always used that word, though she couldn't say why. She feared that someone had planted this device among her things." He pulled a dark and ominous sphere from his jacket. "She had no memory of what it is or how it functions but remained convinced that it posed an extreme danger to her, and to you, so she asked me to hold onto it for her."

Henry watched Allen closely as he cradled the glassy orb in his palm, staring into its depths as if it were a crystal ball that could reveal his future.

"She assured me that it would pose no danger to me, that this button was encoded for her use alone—"

"Though I am certain," Allen said, turning the object over carefully and pressing his own thumb to the button, "that with the proper tools and expertise, one might easily bypass that mechanism. Perhaps by doing so, one could follow her to wherever she disappeared…"

"Allen! Do you hear how ridiculous you sound?"

"Oh, yes. I imagine it would sound rather odd."

"Allen, she even confessed that she suspected she…that she came from a future era." Henry spoke this in a tone barely above a whisper, full of shame for his brother's association with such a woman.

Allen's head snapped up, and his previously dull eyes shone with a new alertness. "The future? Are you referring to *time travel*?"

"You see why I was opposed to her? She was clearly not in her right mind. I only wish I'd warned you sooner to spare you the heartbreak and the soil upon your reputation. I should have had her committed myself." He clicked his tongue, imagining how the other passengers must already be whispering and spreading vicious rumors of the scene Allen had made upon the ship's departure. He had himself to consider, too. After all, who would employ a psychiatrist unable to help his own disturbed brother?

"It all makes perfect sense now," Allen said.

"Fabulous! Then I shall expect you for dinner in the first-class dining saloon in one hour. They're serving your favorite: lobster! And afterward, we can have cigars and enjoy the Turkish Baths. Finally, I shall have agreeable companionship!"

"Yes. Thank you so much, dear brother," Allen said, staring at the orb. "I do owe you."

THE PRESENT

CHAPTER FOUR: APRIL 10, 2012

The spinning slows. Suddenly, everything stops.

My legs flail, searching for solid ground, until I plunge abruptly into dank, smelly water. I gasp, and my mouth fills with brine. I'm being dragged in one direction, but instinct pulls me the opposite way. I kick against my heavy skirts and break the surface. For one dizzying moment I'm utterly confused. The concrete slabs of the nearby docks sharpen my fuzzy memory.

1912.

Southampton.

The *Titanic*.

I Extracted while on the gangplank—a gangplank that doesn't exist in 2012. This is exactly why our travelers are encouraged to use pre-approved Extraction locations. The Wormhole dumps travelers at the same place they've left from, which can make for some awkward (or dangerous) entrances.

Across the way, Marie does a frantic doggie-paddle toward the steel rungs leading up to the dock. With labored strokes, I swim after her, clutching the sphere in one hand. When I reach her, she's still clinging to the bottom rung, too exhausted to climb to safety.

"Hang on." I slip my Wormhole Device into my handbag and

pull my dripping body up to the dock. Water streams out around me, forming a dark puddle on the concrete. The evening sun, balancing on the very edge of the horizon, casts an eerie glow on the water.

"Okay. Come on up—"

My encouragement is drowned out by the sound of retching. *Lovely.*

I clench my jaw to stop my teeth from rattling and focus on retaining my professionalism—not easy, considering the mucked-up circumstances.

Finally, Marie starts up the ladder, ascending tentatively, with gasping breaths. When she's close enough to grab my forearms, I pull her up with much grunting and tugging. Her eyes widen as she takes in the industrial warehouses, giant cranes, and sprawling parking lots that seem to have appeared instantaneously.

"What have you done?" Her voice rises in pitch with each word. She edges up against one of the bollards that so recently moored the great ship. Now it stands abandoned, with orange paint chipping and cracking on its knobby head. Marie leans over it and heaves again. I turn away, my own stomach constricting at the smell.

A few boats are moored further down the dock, but the people aboard them are only shadowy figures, too occupied with their own work to pay attention to us. A handful of dockworkers are scattered around the harbor, each focused on their own tasks. The nearest ones are far enough not to hear our conversation, but if Marie screams, they'll come running. She, too, looks around—probably for an escape route. But we're back now; why is she still determined to run?

It's then that everything falls into place. "You don't remember any of this, do you?"

Could it be that after seven years on the job, *now* I get a Confab? It'd certainly explain a lot. It's an inconvenience for certain, but it's at least a legitimate explanation for how this Retrieval got so out of hand so quickly.

"Remember what?" She cowers like a frightened animal. "Don't come any closer! I'll jump!"

Great. A Confab. Today is not my day.

I retreat a step, holding my hands up, palms out. "I'll stay right here. My name is Elise Morley. I understand you may be confused. I can explain to you what has happened, but first we need to move off this dock."

"What have you done to Allen?"

I lower my arms but keep my distance. In the calmest and most comforting tone I can muster through my chattering teeth, I say, "I'll show you the travel contract and explain everything once we reach a secure location."

"Travel contract? But Allen made all the arrangements." She tucks her arms around herself, as if trying to create a cocoon. "Please, tell me where he is."

I take a deep breath. Step one, find a secure location.

I slide my cell phone from the hidden, waterproof pocket of my handbag where I also keep my modern-day credit card and passport. Travelers are forbidden from taking modern objects into the past, but after spending three weeks stranded in Tibet waiting for my passport, I convinced Dr. Wells to amend the Rule to exclude Retrievers.

I glance around, momentarily forgetting I'm in the present, where modern technology doesn't need to be concealed. My fingers are still numb, so I exhale warm breath onto them until they've thawed enough to text the PITTA headquarters. "Retrieval successful. Lodgings required in Southampton, UK."

Marie watches me, her eyebrows raised at the compact flip phone. I try to remember all my training about Confabs. It seems like eons ago that Dr. Wells put me through the crash-course.

"Do you know what this is?" I hold up the phone.

She shakes her head, but her left eye twitches.

A couple taps later and I have a picture of Marie herself staring back at me from my phone, a microphone in one hand and a coy smile on her heavily-glittered face. I hold it up for her, hoping the visual stimulus will trigger her memory.

"That's me! But...I don't understand." She presses her palms to her temples and squeezes her eyes shut.

"Let's find someplace to talk and I'll explain everything. I promise."

She gazes out over the water, as if expecting Allen to emerge from the waves. I can't blame her for her hesitation. After all, in her mind, I've yanked her away from the man she loves, put her through an excruciating physical experience, and dropped her in the middle of the ocean. It's been a rough day for both of us.

My phone chirps. It's Maggie. According to her text, the nearest hotel is less than a mile away, and she's already reserved two adjoining rooms. Finally, a stroke of luck.

I survey the two of us: sopping wet, bedraggled, and dressed like a bunch of *My Fair Lady* rejects. Henry Higgins would have a field day with us.

A pair of sailors spots us from across the docks. One points at us and—though I can't hear their conversation—their laughter reaches us.

"We need to move." I offer Marie a hand, but she flinches as if I'm something from a nightmare. The men are approaching quickly, but Marie remains stony, like she hasn't heard me at all. "It's going be much colder when the sun goes down. What do you say we find some dry clothes so we don't get hypothermia?"

She glares at me contemptuously, but—after a self-conscious glance at her ruined dress—she squares her shoulders and allows me to help her up. I realize then she doesn't have her Wormhole; she must've dropped it in the harbor. The Object Retrievers won't be happy about having to organize a dive, but at least I know where it is, so they won't have to remote-destroy it.

By the time we reach Canute Road, which leads out of the harbor and into the city, we've lost the sailors. A post-Extraction headache balloons within my brain. I pull a small compact of painkillers from my handbag. Only two left.

"Aspirin?" I offer one to Marie as an olive branch. She takes it hesitantly.

Maggie's wicked web-searching skills serve her well; she has an uncanny knack for finding post-Retrieval lodging that won't draw too much attention to us. Comic book conventions, historical reenactments, Renaissance fairs, movie filming locations, local theater districts…it's amazing how many places exist where a couple of travelers in vintage clothing can blend in.

I lead the way through littered back alleys and side streets, following the directions on my phone. Marie falls behind, forcing me to link arms with her to keep her moving. She stops when she first spots the lines of traffic and again when we walk past a row of parked cars. Pedestrians pass us by, some gawking, but I smile and nod politely, and they leave us be.

When I see the flag with the single white star on the hotel's logo, my mouth goes dry. I push the door open and immediately freeze in place.

The hotel lobby bears an uncanny resemblance to the South Western Hotel's, with neo-classical arches and pillars framing each door. What sets it apart, though, is the collection of pieces depicting an elegant, four-funneled ship. In the center of it all, a sign announces: "*Titanic:* A 100th Anniversary Commemoration."

CHAPTER FIVE: APRIL 10, 2012

Maggie knew what she was doing when she booked us rooms at this hotel. A couple in Victorian eveningwear checks in at the front desk. Two boys in knickers and suspenders, each clutching their mother's hand, point and exclaim at the exhibits. A small army of bellhops wearing vintage suits rolls luggage in and out of the elevators.

It's perfect, except for one complication: Marie.

She stops behind me, backing away from a group of short-skirted teens. The girls giggle and whisper behind their hands. They probably assume we're overzealous history fanatics, which I suppose is true, in a way.

The distraction only lasts a moment. Marie's gaze wanders across the room.

Photographic enlargements and paintings on canvas line the lobby's walls. A half-dozen folding tables, draped with expensive satin tablecloths, hold small-scale models, postcards, and tacky souvenir-shop trinkets with orange price tags. Marie touches a plush toy ship with a quiet reverence, her brow softly furrowing in recognition. A sticker on it says, "squeeze here," and when she does, it emits the harmonic tone of a steam whistle.

I try to steer her to the front desk. Still holding the plush ship, she twists around, trying to shake me off. Suddenly, she stops and her voice catches in her throat with a pitiful, strained half-cry.

She's spotted it.

The stars in the dark sky twinkle and blink on an enormous canvas and reflect up from the sea painted below. Rows of lights still illuminate the ship as it raises its hull into the air. In that moment, it defies gravity, defies belief, defies all the claims that it was "unsinkable." The ocean in the foreground is icy black, overwhelming in its depth and cruelty. In the periphery float the dark shadows of lifeboats, the survivors slumped and defeated, helpless as their husbands, fathers, brothers, and friends cry out from the bleak water.

Marie walks toward the painting, drawn in by it. Her fingers barely brush the canvas as she reaches out to the dark, desperate shadows: half-submerged, stretching out to the sky, calling upon their loved ones, upon God Himself to rescue them.

Then, in one sudden, sweeping movement, her body slumps over. She falls to the floor, knocking her head on the edge of a table on her descent.

A woman shrieks. "She fainted!"

"Mum, is she okay?"

"Someone, call an ambulance!"

"It's okay." I step forward. "I'm a nurse. It's probably just the corset. She's been short of breath all afternoon, but she refused to loosen it."

I check her vital signs as the others look on, muttering with grave expressions. She's breathing normally and her eyelids are starting to flutter, so I call one of the nearby bellhops.

"Could you help me carry her to the room? She needs to remain lying down in a cool and quiet place. We have reservations under the name Morley."

"Sure." He wipes a bead of sweat from his lip. In the process, he knocks his fake mustache askew but doesn't seem to notice.

Marie's eyes spring open. She stares up at the circle of faces with calm curiosity, until her eyes land on mine. Then, she gasps. "I remember!"

"You've had a bit of a fall," I interrupt, "but don't worry. You're fine now. We'll get you up to your room so you can rest. We have to make sure you don't have a concussion. Do you understand?"

All the way up to the room, Marie allows herself to be supported by the two bellhops. Entering the room first, I throw a blanket on the sofa and instruct them to lay her down.

When the bellhops leave, I close the door behind them with a sigh. *What else could go wrong?*

The hotel is one of the most extravagant places I've stayed. There are gilded embellishments around the doors and windows, and soft, luxurious upholstery on the chairs and sofa. On the four-poster bed, crimson pillows with gold fringe and matching blankets are heaped, warm and inviting. My body aches just looking at them.

"Are you feeling any better?" I ask, uncertain if I'm speaking with the 1910s heiress or the 2010s pop star.

"I think so. Just confused."

"Can I get you a cup of coffee?" I stifle a yawn and gesture to the kitchenette. "Or something to eat?"

"Just tea, please." Marie's tone wavers.

After starting the kettle heating, I grab two robes from the bathroom and hang my dress over a towel rack. Maggie will have modern clothes delivered to the hotel room overnight as she always does, but for right now my reflection in the full-length mirror appears regretfully unprofessional in the fuzzy bathrobe. I pull my hair into a bun and try to make the best of it. Anything beats shivering in smelly, wet clothing all night.

"Do you think you can get up?" I ask Marie as I hand her the second robe.

She groans. "I think so."

"I'll be right back with the tea." I duck into the kitchenette to give her some privacy. When I'm sure she's had enough time to pull off her wet clothes, I carry in our mugs of Earl Grey.

She accepts hers, thanking me politely, as if I'm some neighbor who's invited her over for afternoon tea and crumpets. Maybe it's due to the genteel upbringing she's fabricated for herself, but I certainly won't complain about it; I prefer demurely subdued over violently panicked any day.

Settling into an armchair, I place my own tea on the coffee table. Now…where to begin?

"My name is Elise, and I work for a company called Place in Time Travel Agency, or PITTA. Do you remember coming to PITTA?" I pause, gauging her reaction.

She closes her eyes and scrunches up her forehead.

"It's okay," I say. "You won't remember everything all at once. At PITTA, we specialize in providing clients with excursions into the past. We're very selective in our clientele. I understand you were referred by a friend who thought a break from the present might benefit you?"

This time, when Marie opens her eyes, I can see in her expression that she does remember something. "Yeah. I mean, yes." The verbal slip throws her off, and she has to take a deep breath before continuing.

"My manager threw me out of the recording studio. He told me to pull myself together." She stops suddenly, the realization of what she said causing her teacup to rattle in her hand.

"What else do you remember?"

"An older gentleman approached me about the agency. I needed time to clear my head, to distance myself from certain people in my life. So I signed up." Her eyes widen, and I can tell her mind is working at full speed, grasping at the information it had suppressed. "What happened to me?"

"You've experienced something we refer to as confabulation." Marie remains blank-faced, so I continue. "Time travel is a fairly recent development. About a decade ago, Dr. Wells, the head of PITTA, invented the devices we use. This isn't something humans have experienced before, so we don't know precisely how each individual will cope.

"For most people, their minds simply compartmentalize their vacations in the past as something slightly *less* than reality. For them, it's like performing in a play, reading a book, or having a very vivid dream. They may become immersed in the world and caught up in the experience, but their subconscious labels the experience as 'not real,' or at least, not *as* real as the present.

"Occasionally, though, travelers become emotionally invested in the past, and their brains mislabel the *present* as 'not real' and fill in the gaps that would conflict with that conviction. They may give themselves a new identity and a new background story, even a new persona with different habits and preferences. Everything about the present time that isn't blocked out, their mind dismisses as something fictitious they heard somewhere or read or dreamt up."

Retrieval Specialists, of course, are the exception. We travel so frequently that our minds adjust to the reality of both places. In my line of work, the past is just my office. Jumps are just a commute.

"What do I do now?" she whispers, her face suddenly rigid and thoughtful.

"Confabulation like yours occurs very rarely, but you don't need to worry. It's harmless and reversible. Sometimes being back in the present is enough to trigger real memories. Others need a few hours of sleep for the brain to rewire itself, filling in the information about the present that it had previously suppressed. In your case, hitting your head may have jogged your memories."

I watch silently as she struggles to reconcile the two stories—her true history, and the past that her mind had constructed for itself.

"But I know who I am. My name is Marie van Grete. I was born in New York. My father is a well-respected businessman. He sent me to London to stay with my aunt for the spring while he was away on business." She stops, her mouth agape. "I'm sorry. I...I don't know where that came from."

"It's okay. Your mind is still processing the information."

"What about Allen? We were going to be married. It was all arranged. We were planning an autumn wedding. Allen...I...I love him." Her voice cracks and tears well up in her eyes.

I close my eyes, trying not to think about Allen. He saw me Extract, and that kind of slip-up could cost me my job.

"You signed a contract with PITTA for a two-month trip," I say, ignoring her question. "I was sent to Retrieve you when you missed your Extraction deadline, to help guide you back to the present."

"Fine. I understand." She pauses, straightening her robe and rising from her seat. "Now take me back."

"I can't. You belong here."

"No. I belong with Allen." Desperate tears flow freely, painting shiny pathways down her cheeks. "Send me back."

"I can't. You broke the Rules."

"From one woman to another," she says, dropping to her knees at my feet. "You still have your device; you can send me back. I'll meet him in New York and tell him I booked passage on another liner to join him. No one else needs to know."

"Even if I wanted to, I can't. The Wormhole Device doesn't have those capabilities. It's for Extractions only, a tether from the past back to your time of origin. You need much more powerful technology to Jump to another time or place, and that technology's only available back at the agency."

She buries her head in her hands. A pang of sympathy jolts my conscience. I hate being the bearer of bad news, the harbinger of truth sent to shatter her beautiful illusions. Then again, I remind myself, the Rules are there for a reason. It's obvious Marie would do everything she could to go back there and marry her fiancé, without any regard to the effect it may have on the present.

"Can you at least get a message to him?"

I open my mouth to object, to remind her that Allen more than likely perished on the *Titanic*, but quickly snap my jaw shut. It must be difficult to suddenly leave everything you *thought* was your life. She just wants closure. I've put her through enough today; I can give her this tiny sliver of peace, even if it is false.

"I'll see what I can do," I say, though frankly, after what just happened, I'm considering avoiding the Gilded Age entirely from now on. *If* Dr. Wells even allows me to Jump again.

"Tell him…tell him I'll miss our days by the seaside, but that he should carry on and be happy, even if I'm not there."

Her request sounds so melodramatic that I have to stop myself from wrinkling my nose at the unabashed sentimentality. Instead, in an impulsive gesture of sympathy, I put my hand on hers. Regardless of anything else, clearly her feelings for her fiancé were genuine, and the memories they made together won't be easily forgotten.

CHAPTER SIX: APRIL 11, 2012

The warm, caramel-apple sun barely peeks over the Southampton skyline, but the room adjoining mine is already empty. Marie left me a note, two lines that assure me she remembers everything now and that she plans to spend a few days in Europe to clear her head before flying back to America.

I shove the note into the pocket of my new jeans, grumbling to myself that she didn't even bother to hang up her dress. It lies abandoned in a pile on the floor—drenched, smelly and wrinkled. I guess she really was ready to move on.

I take a final look around the hotel room to make sure I haven't left anything behind, and then I'm ready to move on as well.

"Sir, I think your wife would *love* touring the Barbados this time of year." Maggie sits behind PITTA's front desk and pushes colorful travel brochures across to a middle-aged man with a comb-over. "We have an excellent package here, though it doesn't include meals." She leans over the desk and points to the price with a fire engine red fingernail. Even from the doorway, I can see the man's nostrils flare.

Maggie catches me watching and winks. I just shake my head.

People who walk into the front reception often assume the Place in Time Travel Agency is just another overpriced rip-off, but our actual customers—all personal referrals—know to request a trip to Richmond, Surrey when they come in. Only then are they directed back to the *real* travel agency.

Since I'm eager to avoid Maggie and her inevitable questions about my botched Retrieval, I hurry past the tangerine upholstery and gaudy 80s travel posters and slip into the back.

The real travel agency, where we prepare our clients for their exclusive vacations in the past, is a million times brighter, cleaner, and easier on the eyes. And somewhere in here, I'm certain, I can find some aspirin.

Black leather sofas encircle a low coffee table, and on each of the walls is a poster-sized, full-color photograph of a great New York moment: Henry Hudson sailing the *Half Moon* into the harbor, George Washington's inauguration, and the construction of the Empire State Building. Off to one side, a coffeemaker and a pastry tray sit on a counter beside the filing cabinet we affectionately refer to as "The Black Hole." The aspirin is supposed to be kept on top of the filing cabinet but, as usual, is missing. Maybe if I'm lucky it just fell into a drawer.

As I dig elbows-deep into The Black Hole's top drawer, the door to the adjoining room opens. I glance up and smile at the middle-aged man with the gray mop of hair who flops into the armchair. "Hey, Joe."

"Back so soon?" He barely looks up from his paperwork. Today, his forehead seems to contain more ridges than usual, and his permanent grimace turns down at a sharper angle. Even his posture is slouched, creating unseemly wrinkles in his high-end suit.

"Sure am. What's up with you?" I ask cautiously. My fingers close around what might be an aspirin bottle, but it turns out to be a cathode-ray tube from an old TV, so I toss it back in.

"Another 9/11 request." He scowls, flipping through a manila folder. As PITTA's Jump Specialist, Joe's job is to prepare clients for their trips to the past, or—in cases like this—to explain why we won't allow certain Jumps.

I stand on my tiptoes to reach deeper into the cabinet. The aspirin has to be in here somewhere. "Pretty early in the year to be getting September requests, isn't it?"

"Why does no one understand the 'annual interval' thing?" he grumbles. "How hard is it? You leave here April 11 and you arrive there on April 11. The only thing that changes is the year. And then they all want to know why. Do I look like a physics professor?"

Aha! I pull out the aspirin bottle and slam the drawer shut. The stupid childproof cap refuses to budge. "Another hero in the making?" I ask as I fiddle with the cap.

"Aren't they all?" Joe stirs his coffee violently, cursing when it sloshes out of the Styrofoam cup onto his pants. "Every one of 'em insists he's got some sort of brilliant plan that will save the day. Never mind that they'd be breaking nearly every single one of the Rules. Do they even bother to read the Rules?" He dabs at his pants with a napkin, trying to sop up the spilled beverage.

"I wonder that, too, sometimes."

"Oh, they'll agree with all the Rules *in theory*, but every one of them wants us to make an exception in their case. For the greater good, of course."

"Have you heard from the other Retrievers lately?" I ask, popping in a few aspirin and pouring myself a cup of coffee to wash it down. Retrievers come and go so frequently that the others are practically strangers to me. There's one guy, Mike, whom I've only met twice, though he's been here as long as I have. He has the physique of a bodybuilder and specializes in the most dangerous Retrievals, when we have reasons to believe the client might put up a fight. Bob, Tom, and Sam—all pseudonyms, of course—were hired after me, and I don't see any of them more than two or three times a year.

"Well, you just missed Bob. He was stuck here for a month," Joe says. "Dr. Wells needed him to Retrieve someone from the 1340s and it took a while to come up with a vaccination for the Plague. The poor guy was going stir-crazy sitting in one place for so long."

I grin as I sip my coffee. I can relate; I get antsy between assignments, too. The past is often easier to deal with than the present.

"Tom got back a few days ago, too," Joe says, raising his eyebrows. "Messy Retrieval. The guy wanted to prevent Lincoln's assassination. It got ugly. We got him back to the present, but from what I hear, they had quite the skirmish. Tom ended up with a shiner the size of an orange."

"What happened to the client?"

"Same as always...blacklisted, taken care of. He won't cause trouble for us again. When did you say you were again?" Joe asks, finishing off his coffee.

"1912. I had a Confab who forgot about the whole *Titanic* incident. I'm not looking forward to telling Dr. Wells about it."

Joe raises his eyebrows. "Hadn't ever seen the movie, huh? I don't know how you could forget a story like that. And that song..." He starts loudly humming his own rendition of the Celine Dion tune, horribly off-key. I shake my head, knowing he's just putting on an act for me. Nobody could be *that* tone-deaf.

"How do you forget something like that?" he says again. "I wouldn't worry about it, though. You'll be fine. Everyone knows you're the old man's favorite."

It's true, but on the other hand, Dr. Wells *is* a stickler for the Rules. I run my finger around the cup's rim, wondering what I'd do if I were let go. My particular skill set isn't one with a whole lot of uses in the 'real' world. I don't even have a college degree. Ever since striking up a conversation with Dr. Wells at a sci-fi convention seven years ago, my education has been informal, hands-on, and not exactly something I could put on a résumé.

Joe leans forward to roll himself out of the deep chair and grunts to his feet. "Speaking of which, he's been asking after you—I'm surprised he hasn't barged in here already, actually. He's been frantic about something the last couple of days, but he's keeping it all hush-hush."

As if on cue, Dr. Wells bursts through his door, sets his bespectacled eyes on me, and says, "Elise! There you are. Come in, come in."

I shoot a desperate, *help-me-out-here* glance at Joe, who gives me a halfhearted salute as he measures out the ground beans for another pot of coffee.

"See you later," he says, though, as usual, neither of us has any idea when 'later' might be.

CHAPTER SEVEN: APRIL 11, 2012

Dr. Wells exhales as though he's been holding his breath the entire time I was gone. With his stout and rather rotund physical features, he reminds me of Santa Claus. A really brilliant, mad-scientist kind of Santa. He hurries to close the door behind me.

His office is a mystery of the universe, one of those Mary-Poppins-bag places where all the items shouldn't logically fit in such a small space. Calling it cluttered, though, would do a disservice to the astonishing objects housed there. Aside from his scientific inventions lying in various stages of assembly, the shelves on the wall are also packed with historical treasures. Some of our regular clients like to bring back souvenirs for him: Faberge eggs, Nazi gold, a few Monets. It wouldn't surprise me to find the Ark of the Covenant stashed in his closet.

"That's new." I point to an oil painting. "Is that...?"

"Raphael's *Portrait of a Young Man*." Dr. Wells pushes his pudgy lower lip out into a scowl. "I guess we know now where that disappeared to. And here we've been blaming the Nazis for taking it."

"You could forbid the removal of items from the past," I suggest.

Dr. Wells shakes his head; I wonder if he even heard me. A sharp trill of his old rotary phone breaks the silence.

Dr. Wells reaches into one of his piles—a hodgepodge of ancient writing tools and Popular Mechanics magazines—and retrieves a phone receiver with a shaking hand. He glances nervously out the window. Drops of sweat pool on his forehead.

"Yes, she's here. No, no, I haven't told her anything yet. Where? A car? Oh…okay. Yes, sir. Goodbye."

He hangs up and turns to me. "We need to go."

"Okay." His actions are highly irregular, even for him, but Dr. Wells is the kind of person who always knows what he's doing, so I shrug and follow him out the back door.

When the door opens into the bright afternoon sun, a gust of wind blows through the back alley, carrying with it an unfamiliar, musky cologne. I turn and find myself face-to-face with the largest man I've ever seen. He wears an expensive black pinstripe suit, dark shades, and—blending into the shadows of his suit jacket—a military-grade assault rifle.

A scream lodges in my throat, but when Dr. Wells grabs my arm, I swallow it back down, where it rages silently in my chest. The man points us to a dark luxury car with tinted windows.

"What's going on here?" I ask.

The large man opens the vehicle's back door.

"Get in," he says, his voice a deep growl. Dr. Wells complies and gestures for me to follow. With a glare at the giant, I slide into the car's impeccably clean back seat. It smells brand-new.

"Does this have to do with 1912?" I ask.

Dr. Wells shakes his head but remains stone-silent. The trembling of his hands speaks volumes, though.

The door slams shut, startling me. The dark-suited man climbs in the front seat, and the whole vehicle dips with his weight. He twists around, holding out two cups of clear liquid.

"Drink this." It's a command, not a question.

"Are you crazy?" I reach for the door handle. It flips back and forth uselessly; I've been thwarted by the child lock.

Dr. Wells takes both cups. He looks at me with an expression that's a mix of fear and concern, but what worries me the most is that he seems to know what's going on. He places one container in my palm, closing my fingers around it.

"What is it?"

"It's okay, Elise," he says, his voice barely audible. With a deliberate look into the rearview mirror, he turns up one of the cups, swallowing the entire contents in one swig.

"You're sure about this?" I ask. He nods, but his expression doesn't reassure me. It seems I'm without any options.

I throw back the contents of the cup. It's flavorless, except for a slight metallic aftertaste.

I turn to Dr. Wells, but he's no longer awake. Panicked, I touch his neck, searching for a pulse. His heart beats in a calm, steady rhythm.

My mind tells me to fight, but my body moves so slowly. Out the window, the world blurs like watercolors. It reminds me of being in a Jump, and the sense of panic melts away.

I close my eyes.

CHAPTER EIGHT: APRIL 12, 2012

I wake disoriented. My mind snaps back to reality quickly, but my body still feels sluggish.

Once my eyes adjust to the light, I'm strangely disappointed. I don't know what I expected to see—a dungeon with torture chambers? aliens in glass tubes?—but the plain oak table and six cheap office chairs surrounding it are underwhelming and aren't at all in line with the way my heart is pounding. Who kidnaps someone to take them to an office?

With a glance behind me, I quickly adjust my assessment. Our guard is even taller and wider than the driver who picked us up, and his intimidation factor easily makes up for what the room itself lacks. He has at least half a dozen guns and knives strapped to his belt. His eyes shift toward me and I jerk my head down to stare at my toes.

Dr. Wells and I sit side by side, waiting for whatever event this tense preamble has foreshadowed. Suddenly, the guard at the door holds one hand up to his earpiece and says, "Excellent, sir."

When the door opens, a pair of tall, slim, dark-suited men emerges from the hallway. The guards dwarf them physically, but there's something about their movements and the precise angles at which they hold themselves that makes them even more unnerving.

At first glance, they look identical in their Ray-Bans, close-cropped haircuts, and tailored suits, but on closer observation, I realize they're probably not even related. Slight differences in their facial structures jump out—one has a larger nose, the other's hair has a reddish undertone—and I store these in my memory, hoarding them like weapons of defense.

At the sight of the pair, Dr. Wells tenses. In a smooth, coordinated movement, the twins-who-aren't-really-twins simultaneously take their identical seats across from us. The eerie effect sends a shiver down my spine.

"Good afternoon, Miss Morley," the one on the left—Big Nose—says, nodding toward me. "I'm Agent Baker."

"I'm Agent Butcher," the other says in the same deep drone.

I raise my eyebrows, amused despite myself. "Butcher...Baker...what happened to the candlestick maker?"

The agents glare at me, or at least I imagine they do, since I can't see their eyes behind their dark glasses. The identical, severe pursing of their lips warns me they have no intention of allowing anyone to lighten the mood. I open my mouth to apologize, to reassure them that it was a joke, and a *really* bad one at that, probably just brought on by nerves, when Baker says, "That's why we called you in. Agent Chandler has gone AWOL, and you are going to Retrieve him for us."

"What?"

"That's 'absent without leave,'" Butcher says, disdain puncturing each syllable.

"I know what AWOL means. Dr. Wells? What is all this?"

Dr. Wells stares at his hands, refusing to meet my eye.

Butcher interrupts before Dr. Wells can respond. "In recent years, our organization has been very interested in your agency's work."

"You've been watching us?"

"We are currently involved in using your employer's technology to serve a greater purpose but have encountered some complications with Agent Chandler's disappearance. We've been following your cases and believe you are exactly the person we need for this job."

Dr. Wells continues staring into his lap like a kindergarten troublemaker waiting for his parents in the principal's office. What's he gotten us into?

Baker picks up where his counterpart left off. "We've known about the technology at the Place in Time Travel Agency for some time now. In fact, we had your employer here build us our own technology to aid us in our goals."

"And...what goals might those be?" I ask, surprised again at my own boldness. Instead of hiding under the table like I should be or working to maintain my normally level-headed demeanor, I seem to be blurting out the first things that pop into my head.

Get it together, Elise.

"We aid in the protection of citizens," Butcher says.

"Wait..." A realization hits me. "So you're...government?"

I'm usually pretty good at reading people, but their sunglasses are throwing me off. I feel a sudden urge to rip them off their faces, but the giant with the cache of weapons behind me grunts and I remind myself to behave.

"We can neither confirm nor deny our association with the United States government," Baker says. "You're here on a need-to-know basis."

"We'll put this simply, in the interest of time." The corner of Butcher's mouth twitches at his own joke. "Baker, Chandler, and I are in the same line of work as your organization. Only instead of using this profound scientific knowledge for commercial tourism, risking the lives of all of us in the present for the whims of the one percent—" He spits this part out, his disdain apparent even from behind his dark shades. "—we use it for the greater good of *all* people.

"Your employer has an arrangement with us. We allow you to continue running your little sideshow—assuming you keep a close watch on your clients—in exchange for the technology and expertise that allows us to ensure the safety of our future."

"But that's impossible," I say. "Dr. Wells has proven it's impossible to Jump forward."

Butcher and Baker smirk, an eerily identical twitch that only tugs at one corner of their mouths. Some distracted part of my brain registers that Baker has a dimple where Butcher does not, but the gravity of the situation quickly jerks me back.

Dr. Wells lied to us. He lied to *me*.

Out of the corner of my eye, I catch him squirming uncomfortably. If it were anyone else, I'd be furious, but Dr. Wells is the one person in the world I can't ever seem to get mad at. My heart immediately jumps to his defense. He *must* have had some good reason for keeping this a secret.

"We investigate major plans of action—legislative bills, large corporate dealings, and the like—using the devices that Dr. Wells has built us. We Jump forward to see what effect each action will have on the future. From there, we can guide the path of events, either by blocking legislation, buying out companies, or advising major players in the proceedings to protect our future. We operate under the pseudonym of TUB: the Trial Undertaking Bureau."

That explains the Butcher, Baker, and Chandler pun. Who knew covert government agencies had a sense of humor?

"So you're telling me there are alternate future timelines? Parallel universes? Everett's many-worlds interpretation?"

As a Retriever, my priority has always been to ensure the integrity of our present timeline, to make sure clients don't alter history. I've always operated on the assumption that the way things had happened were the way things were *supposed* to happen, and any alterations would be...well, *wrong*, and potentially dangerous. Travel to the future was never a variable I had considered, and now my mind spins, trying to sort through the implications.

"The choices we make today will affect the future, and it's our duty to determine which of those choices is best."

"What about democracy? Free will?" What would the freedom-loving citizens of America think if they knew the biggest decisions in our country are being determined by this bizarre precognition?

"We operate within the system. We're simply using the available resources to ensure we make the most educated decisions possible."

I have a bad taste in my mouth and could really use a drink of water...not to mention a few hours of sleep to let this all sink in. "Can I use the restroom?"

My request is met with a moment of silence before Butcher concedes. The giant guides me down the hall to a washroom and stands at attention outside the door. The tiny, sterile bathroom feels as claustrophobic as the conference room was, but at least I've distanced myself from the agents' suffocating presence.

I wave my phone in the air but can't get a signal in this concrete bunker. I climb up onto the edge of the sink, holding the phone as high as I can, hoping for even one bar. *Blast it.* Maybe I should've upgraded to one of those fancy new smart phones.

Not that there's anyone I could call, anyway. My only relative, an estranged brother, knows nothing about my work, and any of the other Retrievers would love an opportunity to Jump guns-a-blazing into the future on a secret rescue mission. Aside from that, any acquaintances—neighbors, high school friends, and the like—I've purposely kept at an arm's length for years, a necessity when spending so much time in the past.

My work with PITTA has created such distance between me and everyone else in my life that I don't have anyone to turn to. I hop down and splash my face with cold water, willing myself to stop wallowing and focus on the task at hand.

Back in the conference room, I know what's coming: the details of my mission. Before agreeing to anything, though, I need to talk to Dr. Wells. Even his evasiveness today and his past lies don't negate the fact he's the only confidante I have right now. When I make the request to speak with him alone, the agents nod knowingly, as if they've been expecting it.

"So...Doc?" I ask. "What's really going on?"

When he speaks, his words are slow and deliberate. "Elise, I know this isn't what I hired you for. Jumping forward is different, and I honestly don't know how this is all going to work out." His brow furrows and he looks as if he's about to cry. This confrontation would be a whole lot easier if I could bring myself to be mad at him.

I reach out to squeeze his arm, to reassure him I don't think any less of him, although I wonder if perhaps I should. As I lean in, he reaches his arm around me and pulls me in for a full-on bear hug. My muscles tense.

"The room's bugged," he whispers directly into my ear.

I pull away, and as he meets my eye I'm stricken by the terror in his gaze. He clears his throat. "We must cooperate with TUB. They've provided us with certain protections in the past from people with more dangerous motives."

"You mean terrorists?"

"Terrorists...and overambitious men who want to alter the timeline. TUB also helps us take care of clients who become...problematic."

He looks at me pointedly.

Joe's response to my question earlier today pops into my head: *"Same as always...blacklisted, taken care of. He won't cause trouble for us again."*

I've been incredibly, stupidly naïve. How much of what PITTA does has been hidden from me?

Butcher and Baker burst through the door, urging me to sit so we can continue our debriefing. I resist, frozen in place, and the guard shoves me into the seat. For the rest of the discussion, he hovers next to me, his rifle's muzzle gleaming in my peripheral vision.

"Are you ready to cooperate?"

I have no choice. It doesn't matter how much I believe in

democracy and free will and the Constitutional rights of the people and the Star-Spangled Banner and warm apple pie and all of those inspiring, patriotic American sentiments. The decisions have already been made, the deeds already done, and I'm helplessly ensnared in the middle of it all.

It's just a Retrieval, I tell myself, *just like any other.*

Maybe Agent Chandler has just broken or misplaced his Wormhole. Maybe he's waiting out there in the future, anxious to return to the present. After it's all over, *then* I can worry about all the moral implications. For now, I need to survive this.

"Fine," I say. "Tell me about this job."

CHAPTER NINE: APRIL 12, 2012

After the debriefing, I'm taken to a holding room. It wasn't designed for comfort. Between the ash-gray concrete walls and the armed guard outside the metal door, I'm trapped. There's a bed in one corner and a counter with a sink and a mini fridge in the other. A small adjacent room has been furnished with a toilet and a claw-footed tub. It was obviously added as an afterthought, as it's the only thing in the entire area that looks new or clean.

The whole thing reminds me of a castle dungeon. In fact, it bears a striking resemblance to a 13th century prison I recently had to break into on a Retrieval. The client had attracted the attention of a married nobleman and was imprisoned for witchcraft by his jealous wife. Fortunately, the guard had been willing to let me in for a small bribe, and from there, we Extracted away.

I wish I could Extract my way out of here.

The florescent lights emit an incessant buzz, and I still can't get any signal on my cell phone. I sigh. Might as well make the best of it.

I grab a soda from the fridge—not my caffeine of choice, but it'll do—and lower myself into a steaming-hot bath, eager to wash off the grimy feeling that's been clinging to me since setting foot in this building. After drying and throwing my clothes on, I slip into the other room and find, much to my delight, that someone's left me a backpack.

It contains not only the hard copies of the case files I was promised (they must not trust me with a computer) but also a new toothbrush, a single-serve packet of instant coffee, a carton of Easy Mac, and an MP3 player full of '90s grunge music. Despite my travels, there's a special place in my heart for my own generation's music, and somehow, the distorted guitar riffs and emotionally charged angst always remind me of home.

"Thank you, Dr. Wells," I mutter.

I put the headphones on and run the water until it's as hot as I can get it, then concoct the instant coffee in a flimsy paper cup. The room lacks a table, so I balance the drink between my knees and sit on the edge of the bed, pulling out the bulky file with "CLASSIFIED" printed on it in thick, red ink. I scoff. If I were in charge of top secret info, I'd mark it "BILLS" or "TAXES" or "INVENTORY OF AUNT MARGE'S CERAMIC FIGURINES" instead. You mark it as "CLASSIFIED" and of course people are going to want to peek.

The top page includes a photograph, the caption confirming that it's an image of Agent Chandler. He looks nothing at all like Agents Butcher and Baker. He's smiling, for one, and his unruly hair is blonde. I wonder if this was taken before he became an agent and if when he signed on he had to cut and dye his hair and vow to hide behind those infernal sunglasses for the rest of his life. Seems like the kind of thing this humorless organization would do.

The file has been marked up rather brutally, and no amount of squinting allows me to decipher what was printed underneath the dark, black slashes. There's obviously a *lot* that TUB doesn't want me to know. What I'm left with are mere fragments, scraps and hints of the previous life of Agent Chandler: an Ivy League alumnus with master's degrees in computer science and cyber security, as well as a PhD from MIT. He was hired by TUB about two years ago and isn't much older than I am.

I check my watch and curse the time. I'm going to need more caffeine. The pile of information on my lap is simultaneously overwhelming and underwhelming, and my coffee has disappeared. I can't remember the last time I felt so ill-equipped, though it was probably back in high school, back when pop quizzes involved simpler things, like verb conjugations or algebra.

What I can decipher between the obscured lines reveals that Agent Chandler has been in the year 2112 for six months. Even looking at the dates on the page makes my stomach lurch.

Chandler originally arrived in October 2111 to research an immigration issue and was supposed to check in every two months. He checked back in December, but missed February's scheduled Extraction. I gnaw a fingernail, a habit I gave up long ago but which still resurfaces when I'm particularly stressed. TUB should've sent a Retriever months ago. With the length of time he's been gone, *anything* could've happened to him. He could be anywhere. He might even be dead. Why have they waited so long to send someone?

The next papers contain descriptions of electronic retina scanners that allow people of the future to access everything from libraries to healthcare to transportation to bank accounts and specs for some eyeglasses that function as personal computers. I skim over the technical jargon. What I really need is to figure out how to access food and shelter while I'm there.

Fortunately, it seems Chandler has already found a loophole. According to his report, the system operates on credit, but there's a lag in the bureaucratic system that enables invalid retina scan to go unnoticed for seven to ten days.

It seems like a pretty major flaw to me, but at least it takes care of one concern. I hope a week is enough time to hunt down Agent Chandler and that they don't change to a more efficient system in the meantime.

The final page is blank, save for the handwritten words: *The choices you make dictate the life you'll lead.* A lot of good that does me.

I throw the folder down in frustration. TUB's reports contain none of the information I *really* need: where Agent Chandler is lodging, what he's researching, any motives he might have for missing his scheduled Extraction. I need to know where to find food, shelter, and other supplies in this unfamiliar time. I need maps, transportation schedules, information about cultural differences. I'm about to flip through the files again when my music cuts out in the middle of a fantastic guitar solo.

"Hey!" My protest echoes in the sparsely-furnished room. I check the MP3 player, but it still has battery. In fact, according to the display screen, "The Beginning is the End is the Beginning" is still playing.

"Elise," a familiar voice speaks into my ear. "I apologize for my destruction of this file. I have an important message, but TUB can't know I've told you."

It's Dr. Wells. I stare down at the papers, trying to hide my surprise, in case my room is being monitored.

"I have to keep this short, but you need to know what's at stake. You were not the first Retriever assigned this mission. Mike Jumped to the future and returned a few weeks ago. Apparently, Agent Chandler became upset and smashed the extra Wormhole Mike brought for the Extraction. Mike had to return for a replacement, and TUB insisted on holding him overnight. The next morning—" Dr. Wells' voice chokes up, and he clears his throat.

"The next morning he was gone. I tracked his watch's GPS, and two days ago we uncovered his remains."

I shuffle the papers in my lap to cover the trembling of my hands.

"There are things about the mission that TUB doesn't want you to know," Dr. Wells' voice says, "things they don't want *anyone* to know. Please, promise me that if *anything* goes wrong, you'll run. Remain in the future, if you must, but unless you bring Agent Chandler with you, it won't be safe to return."

CHAPTER TEN: APRIL 13, 2012

The next morning the guard leads me to a different room, one that mimics our time lab back at PITTA. Standing in the center is a DeLorean Box. Until yesterday, I thought the only one in existence was at our headquarters. Finding out there's another hidden away in some secret bunker is disconcerting, and there's something about it, sitting here in this strange place, that makes it seem like an evil doppelganger.

I approach it reverently, its hum drawing me in like a mythical siren's song. I brush my fingers over its smooth, silver metal and flawless glass surfaces. It resembles its namesake in its coloring and its sharp, modern angles but is more like the TARDIS than Marty McFly's car—except for the "bigger on the inside" part. The rectangular prism really is only about seven feet tall and three feet in width and depth, whether you're standing inside or out. The door swings open like a shower stall, and opposite that, a string of dials are already set to coordinate the Jump time and location.

Below the panel, a larger dial and digital display indicate the destination year. In our DeLorean Box, that number doesn't go any higher than 1980, but in this one, the dial already indicates the year

2112. The number looks unnatural, an abomination that's too large and strangely intimidating.

"Are you ready?"

I note the silent question hidden beneath Dr. Wells' spoken one.

"It'll be okay," I say. "It's a Retrieval like any other. I'll Jump there and bring this Agent Chandler back where he belongs. Easy-peasy."

My words seem to reassure him, but my own emotions are still a nauseating mix of excitement and trepidation. On impulse, I reach out and grab his hand. In a way, he's become like family to me—like a grandfather, uncle, or that one crazy relative who shows up at Thanksgiving, whose exact place on the family tree is fuzzy, but who's always there, familiar and consistent.

Hearing twin footsteps enter the room, I pull away and use every ounce of mind over matter to put on a brave face.

Butcher holds out an androgynous, flowing, one-piece suit and some matching socks and boots. I raise my eyebrows, but he simply points to an adjoining room.

The suit's inner layer is breathable like cotton, with a soft, cloud-like texture. The outer layer, however, is some sort of synthetic—slightly sticky and rubbery, but with a metallic sheen. It has amazing elasticity but still hangs on my frame like a drape. The boots hug my feet, creating a perfect fit. Though the outfit is comfortable, it's too foreign to me. Frankly, I'd rather wear a corset.

There's no mirror, but I'm certain I look ridiculous walking back into the time lab. The suit's legs and sleeves have been hemmed, but I can't imagine a world where a costume like this would help me blend in. For one irrational second I wonder if this is an elaborate prank. If so, now would be the time for someone to jump out and laugh. *Oh, boy! We really had you going, huh?*

The stern faces that greet me confirm none of these three men have any sense of humor right now.

"Agent Chandler brought that suit back from his last Jump," Butcher says. "You should be able to wear it without drawing attention. You'll need these as well."

He hands me a pair of eyeglasses with silver rims. "They're already configured to your retina scan, so you can use them right away. They're called PVDs—personal visual devices."

I consider asking how they obtained a scan of my retinas, but does it really matter? They probably know more about me than I do.

"You've studied Agent Chandler's files?" Baker asks.

I try to respond, but my tongue sticks to the roof of my mouth and I can't pry my teeth apart, so I just nod.

"We've entered the coordinates of his last known location." Butcher's face twitches slightly, a momentary fracture of his stoic demeanor, brought on by what? Anger? Irritation? Something else?

He hands me two Wormhole Devices. I almost protest. I always use the same Wormhole each time I Jump. It's kind of like a bowler always using the same bowling ball—part superstition, part comfort in the familiar. Mine has a small, but distinct scratch below the thumbprint scanner, but these two are identical, with no distinguishing marks at all. When I look up at the agent, at his stony features and his commanding stance, I swallow my objection.

"You'll need to use TUB's devices for this Retrieval, since you're leaving from their DeLorean Box," Dr. Wells says quietly. "Also, their Wormholes utilize some new technology to make Extractions safer."

"What do you mean? What does it do?"

"Instead of the Wormhole Extracting you to your current location as you're used to, our devices are programmed to transport you back to a predetermined location: TUB headquarters. We can't take any chances," Butcher says. I catch his drift; they want to be the first to know when we Extract back.

"This one is yours." Dr. Wells points to the one in my right hand. "The other is for Agent Chandler."

"Got it," I say, tucking them into separate pockets so I'll be able to keep them straight.

"The DeLorean Box is programmed for you to arrive on April 13, 2112," Butcher says. "We'd have preferred to send you to February of that year, when our agent first went missing, but—"

"I know how the annual interval works." Their insistence on sending a Retriever now, instead of simply waiting until next February is curious, but I don't dare question it.

Butcher glowers at me. "We expect you back within a week's time."

I'd already figured on a week, based on Agent Chandler's notes about the retina scan, but the deadline still makes me nervous. With my limited knowledge, having only seven days to track him down and complete the Extraction might prove difficult.

I nod again to appease the agents and step gingerly into the DeLorean Box. I clench the handrails' heavy-duty rubber grips, carefully testing out the Box to see if feels like the one I'm used to. The numbers "2112" glare up at me menacingly.

Standing there, frozen in anticipation in my silvery one-piece suit as the countdown continues, I feel like an astronaut being launched into space.

"Five...four...three..."

Has man made it back to the moon by 2112?

"Two..."

Do astronauts ever get this same ache in their lungs during lift-off, fearful they'll never find their way back through the darkness?

"One..."

Jumping is an entirely different experience than Extraction. While the Wormhole spins and twists the traveler around like a fish on a line, fighting what Dr. Wells describes as "time resistance," the DeLorean Box provides a smoother ride, like the gut-wrenching drop of a rollercoaster.

Without even opening my eyes, I know the DeLorean Box has vanished around me. I've grown used to the way that, throughout the Jump, I can still feel the handrails, but if I were to look down at my hands (which I don't recommend; it's a surefire way to lose your lunch), I would only see brilliant lights flashing around my body and my fingers gripping thin air as I speed toward the future.

CHAPTER ELEVEN: APRIL 15, 2012

Allen

Brine flooded his throat, filling his airways as the bright light assailed him. For one frantic moment, Allen wondered if heaven really ought to be so wet. Then his head broke the water's surface, and his frenzied sputtering gave way to bursts of crisp, clean air and blinding daylight. The water was chilly, but not the ice-filled terror he'd anticipated. All that remained of that nightmarish scene was the ocean itself, now an innocent blanket spread out before him. He grabbed for the edges of his bulky floatation vest.

It was then he realized that he still clutched the miraculous device in his hand. He blinked at it as he treaded water, shocked at what had occurred. Throwing his head back, he let out a triumphant cry and reveled in the wonders of science. And all he'd had to do was disable the lock.

"Hey! Someone's down there!"

Allen twisted to look over his shoulder. A boat! By some miracle, there was a massive ship not twenty strokes from where he'd landed. What marvelous luck!

"Man overboard!"

Allen floundered in the vessel's choppy wake, his vest thumping against his chin. Though this boat was similar in size to the leviathan he'd just left, its silhouette was sleeker without the four giant funnels perched atop. Obviously, it was not steam-powered. The name *BALMORAL* was stenciled in black letters near the bow.

Someone aboard tossed him a white and orange ring that bobbed across the water's surface. With numb fingers, he wedged the dark orb into his jacket, where it crumpled the now-drenched letter already folded there. Hand over hand, he pulled himself to the lifeline. His teeth chattered. How could anyone have survived that horrific night he'd left behind? Even here, the ocean's chill would have quickly dulled his mind and numbed his body into submission had it not been for the *Balmoral*'s rescue.

Once on deck, a crowd had gathered, and Allen scowled at this unseemly entrance. A sailor draped a heavy blanket over his shoulders. "Don't want you to get hypothermia. Lucky it's been such a warm spring."

Allen straightened up, grateful for his height. Towering over the crowd restored some of his self-assurance. Most of the passengers were well-dressed—the men in suits and top hats, the women in lavish gowns—but there was something about their hairstyles, their shoes, the smallest of details that just seemed peculiar.

"Thank you all for your assistance. Now, if I might—" Allen threw his arm out to steady himself, suddenly overcome with dizziness and fatigue.

"Get him down to the infirmary," the captain ordered, shaking his head. He turned to the crowd. "Excitement's over, folks. Poor guy must've had too much champagne. Please remember to drink responsibly."

The crowd tittered with laughter and turned back to their deck chairs and shuffleboard.

Two sailors—one supporting each arm—guided Allen into the depths of the ship. "We'll have the ship's doctor check at you. The memorial service will be starting in about ten minutes, but you might be able to catch the end if he gives you the okay."

"Memorial service?"

One of the sailors shot an amused look at his shipmate. "How much champagne do you suppose he had?"

Allen didn't respond, for something in a room they'd just passed had caught his eye. The double-doors stood propped open, and beyond them was an elegant dining room set for dinner. Beyond the tables, however, was a life-sized reproduction of the *Titanic*'s very own Grand Staircase, adorned with a banner declaring, "*Titanic* 100th Anniversary Commemoration Cruise." A pair of heavyset women posed before a photographer with wide smiles on their faces, and Allen stared in shock at the trousers the female photographer wore. Before he could even decide which part of the scene he found more distasteful, the sailors had urged him onward.

The infirmary was a sterile, white room with harsh lighting across the ceiling that illuminated the space with the flick of a switch. Beside the cot was a cabinet with the most fascinating instruments Allen had ever seen. Perhaps he'd just feign illness for the rest of the trip so he could study them at his leisure.

The sailors helped him with his life preserver and shoes, but Allen protested when they reached for his jacket, insisting he remove it himself.

"The doctor will be right in," one of them said, shrugging.

Allen nodded, eager for them to leave so he could investigate his surroundings. As soon as they did, he got up and looked around. Beside a large box with an opaque glass front, he found a ballpoint pen and a sheet of paper with the ship's letterhead on top. It reminded him that, as a man of science, he ought to be documenting his experience.

With painstaking care, he unfolded the saturated letter from his jacket pocket and lovingly smoothed it out on his lap. Many words had bled away, but Allen copied them one by one onto a dry page.

When he finished, he palmed the glorious, miraculous sphere in one hand and added a second note to the same page, describing his newest adventures and reassuring his beloved darling that nothing could stop him now. No matter what, he would find her.

THE FUTURE

CHAPTER TWELVE: APRIL 13, 2112

My body jerks to a halt.

Something's wrong. The light piercing my closed lids is too intense. I try to squint but am forced to squeeze my eyes shut again. The sun feels warmer and brighter than it should. I throw one arm out in front of me and step forward. My stomach lurches, gurgles. Feeling around blindly, I find a wall directly behind me, as slick as glass. I lean against it and slide to the ground, clutching my middle.

From the safety of my crouched position, I focus on my other senses. I take in the hurried chatter and steady footsteps but catch no discernible smells, even when I inhale deeply. Someone stops and asks, "Hey, are you okay?" I nod and wave them away.

Through squinted eyes, I can see white-booted feet rushing past me, some balancing expertly on silver-white discs. These cheerfully humming machines are shaped like the saucers I used to slide down Grandpa's sledding hill on every winter, just slightly smaller. Some people stand on them, carefully bracing themselves with one foot in front of the other, hovering over the ground as if by magic. Other discs float further from the ground with seated riders leaning back in ease as they zoom around the city. They look so silly, so ridiculously *sci-fi* that I nearly laugh aloud at the absurdity.

Slowly, my eyes adjust to a world of bright silver and white, reflecting off rows of domed buildings. They all look identical to me, with shiny, reflective glass that makes me feel like I'm trapped in a funhouse of soap bubbles.

Where am I?

The sky is so blindingly bright I can barely lift my gaze above the heads of the passers-by, even when I shield my eyes with my hand. Fortunately, though, the people themselves seem refreshingly normal, except that each wears a pair of silver-rimmed glasses. No cyborg limbs. No bizarre mutations. They even seem to be speaking in languages I can understand.

I push myself to my feet and pull the glasses from my pocket. Rows of miniscule buttons line the edges of the frames, but as much as I press and turn them, I can't get them to do anything. Without knowing how to use them, they're pretty useless, but when in Rome... I set them on my face.

I can do this.

Styles may have changed and transportation may be different, but the ground beneath my feet is still the same Earth I've been exploring for the past twenty-five years. I wiggle my toes, testing the future's solidity. The pavement here reminds me of a ceramic vase: hard, glazed, and pale.

I slowly begin my surveillance. Each building has a revolving door, and I remember reading somewhere that they are the most energy-efficient entryway. I guess our collective descendants finally got serious about conservation.

Each entryway is labeled with bold, black letters, but I don't recognize any of the names until I see one that says "McDONALD'S." Without the trademark golden arches towering above, the word itself seems meaningless. In fact, this whole future seems a large-scale version of that—familiar things taken so far out of context they lose all meaning.

First things first: I need to orient myself. If I can find a map, I can begin to narrow down where I'll be most likely to find Agent Chandler. And where better to find information than a library?

For millennia, humanity has gathered their written records into libraries, and I've seen the best of them, from the Library of Alexandria to the Yunju Temple to the Library of Congress. They've helped me out on numerous occasions in scrounging up essential information and never fail to make me feel safe and contented, at least for a little while. What are the chances that in the next hundred years these gathering places of knowledge would have disappeared completely?

The blue "LIBRARY" sign greets me like an old friend, and I slide through the revolving doors, eager to inhale the familiar stacks of books and—

I stop short.

A man bumps into me, muttering a muffled "*pardón*" as he brushes past. I remain frozen to the spot.

I stare in disbelief, scanning every inch of the building for some sign of well-worn paperbacks or tried-and-true hard covers or even a picture book. All I see, throughout the entire domed building, are aisles and aisles of computer screens. A hundred years isn't enough time to lose our connection to paper, is it? Even as I approach the librarian's desk, I'm still not sure how to phrase my request.

"Excuse me," I say quietly. "I need help finding some information."

The librarian looks about my age, and on the lenses of my glasses, the letters MYAH—her name?—materialize above her head.

She raises her eyebrows at me and points to the computer screens with one slim finger.

"Are there any paper books here?" I ask, cutting to the chase, despite the risk that I might be exposing my ignorance.

She sighs, the heavy sigh of someone who's exasperated and

doesn't care who knows. "You haven't been to the library at all since we left?"

I hesitate, unsure how to answer. Left? "No. No, I haven't. Do you have some maps or books about this place's recent history?" I hope I've chosen my words carefully enough so I don't arouse too much suspicion.

"The *Continuum*'s recent history?"

"Um, yes?"

"You have to sign in on a screen." Myah sighs again and leads me to one of the computers. "You can view it on there or on your glasses for more privacy. You just need to scan to log in. Input what you want to know and the screen will display the information. I'll be at my desk if you need any help."

With the way she mumbles off the directions and hastily retreats to her desk, I doubt she'd be much help if I did ask. I lean forward and tip my PVD to scan my retina. It must work, because a message appears on the screen in front of me:

WELCOME TO THE CONTINUUM LIBRARY, DIPLOMAT GUEST.

Diplomat guest? I wait for something else to happen, but nothing does.

I stare blankly at the screen. I've never been in a situation like this before, where I'm the one behind the times, wondering how technology works and how I'm supposed to use the machines and conveniences that everyone else deems commonplace. I can use an astrolabe. I know Morse Code. Heck, I can even churn butter. But here, in this bookless library, staring at this welcome screen, I feel completely, utterly lost.

"You look lost."

I swivel the chair around and nearly lose my balance when I see who's spoken. The man looks exactly like his picture, and behind his own silver spectacles, his blue eyes study my features just as intently.

Agent Chandler.

Could it really be this easy? I've found him before I even had a chance to start looking. Or has he found me?

My hand falls to my lap, to the pocket of my suit—the suit *he* brought back from this time—and my fingers close around one of the Wormhole Devices. No, this place is much too public, with far too many witnesses. I can't complete the Extraction here. I can't risk that again. A brief glance at Chandler's towering frame is enough to conclude that there's no way I could catch him if he chose to run or force him into an Extraction if he fought it. I need to tread carefully. Play it smart.

"You startled me." I try to act as casually as possible. I turn to the screen, so as not to give anything away with my expression. I release the Wormhole and pull my hand out of my pocket.

"That computer seems to be giving you a hard time. It takes a while to figure out. Personally, I don't know how they can call it a library without any books; it's a like a McDonald's that doesn't serve burgers. What were you trying to look up?"

The question catches me off guard. "Do you work here?"

"No. My name's Chandler. I work for a branch of the Governing Committee. I'm not really allowed to discuss my work. I just happen to like libraries." It's a lie wrapped around the truth, a method I often employ myself.

"I'm Elise. I was just trying to do some research on recent history. About the *Continuum*," I add boldly.

His look bores into my head. He suspects something. I tense, ready for what, I don't know, but then he turns to the screen and starts waving his hands in front of it in a rapid succession of taps and sweeps.

"Here." He hits a final spot on the screen and gestures grandly.

The screen shows a sleek, silver, M&M-like shape hovering against a backdrop of black with white, unblinking stars. I scoot my chair closer, trying to make sense of what I'm seeing. It has a dark, solid-looking bottom half and a top half constructed from glass panels that arch across its circumference. A crisscrossing web of supports holds up each panel.

Words fly across the screen, each a label for a particular section:
"WATER TREATMENT AND STORAGE"
"OXYGEN STORAGE"
"LABORATORIES"
"RECYCLING"

The image spins and twirls in the virtual sky, and I grab the edge of the desk to steady myself. Suddenly, the ground beneath my feet doesn't feel so firm after all. TUB's "improved technology" and their insistence that I use a Wormhole that Extracts directly back to their headquarters makes far more sense now. An image flashes through my head: myself, with Chandler in tow, Extracting out into the vacuum of space. I shiver.

"A beauty, isn't she?" Chandler grins, looking over my shoulder. "So, you wanted to know more about our history?"

He hits a few more buttons and reaches for my ear. I flinch.

"Whoa, relax! I was just going to flip on your PVD's speakers. They look new; have you figured out how to use the speakers yet?"

"I'm technologically illiterate," I say, which is true enough.

He presses a tiny button on the rim of the glasses. My head vibrates with the sound of light, tinny music, like the kind they use in Discovery Channel documentaries. A bold voice interrupts my thoughts.

"In response to increased pressure from environmentalists in the mid-21st century, the United States led the charge on a monumental project, with significant financial backing from national, private, and corporate investors from around the world. It was the most extensive worldwide project ever attempted, with over 85% of nations involved on some level. During the late part of that century, the people of the world worked together to construct a miracle. In April 2110, the *Continuum* was completed: the world's first self-sustaining space colony.

"This colony is home to 20,000 citizens from around the world who have volunteered to participate in this multi-quadrillion dollar experiment. After rigorous screening, these individuals and families were chosen by lottery in what immediately became the world's most-viewed video feed. For the next fifty years, these everyday people will live and work onboard the *Continuum*, surviving off the power of the sun and the food they grow themselves, along with a limited number of provisions brought with them in the shuttles that delivered them to their new home."

The screen becomes fuzzy in my unfocused vision as I try to imagine what would make someone want to leave Earth, to completely desert everything and everyone they knew, and agree to join such an insane venture.

"We're kind of crazy, aren't we?"

I start, so caught up in my own thoughts that I'd forgotten all about Chandler.

"Yeah." I pull my wandering thoughts into check. "So, how'd you end up here, anyway?"

"Luck of the draw, just like everyone else. I've wanted to live on the *Continuum* since I first heard about it. How amazing is it to be the next step in humanity? Did you hear they finally decided on names for the next colonies?"

"No, I must've missed that."

"The *Independence* and the *Vitality*. A little unoriginal, if you ask me, but, hey, that's democracy. Apparently the lotteries for citizenship have already reached three times the number of applicants the *Continuum* had."

"People must be pretty excited."

"Why wouldn't they be? It's like our own little planet: self-sustaining, eco-friendly, low crime rate. It could be the solution to the world's overpopulation problems."

I hadn't expected him to be so passionate about the topic, but then again, he'd probably known what he was getting into, unlike me. I hadn't even known I'd be in space. But why not? Was I really supposed to believe TUB had just *happened* to overlook that detail?

"What about you?" he asks. "How'd you end up here?"

"My boss encouraged me to volunteer." We're both skilled in this truth-in-the-lies dance.

He nods and clears his throat. "Hey, it was nice meeting you. Do you think you could maybe give me your phone number or email address and we could go out for a cup of joe sometime?"

I hesitate, mentally panicking. This is *not* how a Retrieval is supposed to go. On the other hand, if I lose him now, it might be difficult to find him again. Maybe a coffee date isn't such a bad idea. Granted, I don't have a phone number or email address in this era. "Actually, can I have yours? I, ah…"

"Don't have one?" He leans and drops his voice. "Since phone numbers have been defunct since the 2060s and email hasn't been used since the 2080s? And, by the way, no one—at least not around here—has used the word 'joe' for coffee in the past forty years."

CHAPTER THIRTEEN: APRIL 13, 2112

"How did you know?" I ask as we head out the door into the blinding light, all pretenses instantly dropped.

"The blank look on your face when you pulled up the screen, for one." He laughs. "Secondly, you don't exactly strike me as the diplomat type. And, third, let's just say I've seen a watch like yours before."

I grab my PITTA-issued watch, a mixture of terror and fury rising within me before I can take a deep breath and calm myself. After all, Chandler hadn't known TUB would kill Mike for failing to Retrieve him. Or had he?

Chandler strides along, perfectly at ease in this strange city. He points out the sights but keeps his voice soft and low, as if conscious of all the people around us.

"Did you notice the panels? Oh, here, let me fix your PVD." He reaches over to tap a few places on my glasses. "Better?"

"Thanks." Whatever he'd hit had tinted the lenses so that now I can look directly upward toward the structure's crisscrossing panels.

"The panels work on a timer," he says, "blocking more light at night and less during the day. They have to keep it like a sauna in here for the crops in the agricultural district to grow, which is—of course—essential for oxygen and food production. But since everyone wears their PVDs all the time anyway, the light's intensity isn't an issue.

"The buildings," he continues, pointing now at the domed structures, "are constructed with the same plastic material as the roofing panels, and are tinted to reflect light so that it's dimmer and cooler indoors."

I nod, interested in the topic, but uncomfortable at how he's taken complete control of the situation. I hadn't expected to run into him so soon, and I certainly hadn't expected him to volunteer as my personal tour guide. I'd anticipated a few days to get my feet underneath me, survey my surroundings, and come up with an *actual* plan.

"Here we are." He motions to a building with a black sign indicating "COFFEE." "This place isn't too bad; their coffee is the closest to what we're used to. Some of the newer places have some crazy flavors. I tried a cheeseburger macchiato once; it's not nearly as good as it sounds."

He guides me into the revolving doors, and I brace myself, not sure what to expect. A soothing ambiance of warm earth tones greets me, and my shoulders drop in relief. This could easily be a coffee shop in my present-day New York, except for the computerized order screens and the names floating above each barista's head—courtesy of my PVD.

"Retro coffee shops are in style," Chandler says. Smooth jazz wafts from the speakers. I think it's Kenny G, which is a bit anachronistic with the rest of the décor, but besides that, they've done a fine job making it feel very "early 21st century."

"I come here when I get nostalgic." Chandler gestures to a round, wooden table in a quiet corner. "I'll buy."

His behavior is curious, but I don't feel threatened, so I sit. At the front counter, Chandler places the order, leaving me to rein in my thoughts. There are a million questions I need to ask, and they all bombard my mind at the same time. He returns with our coffee—hot steam rising lazily from the cups—before I can even prioritize them.

"I've decided to stay here," he says abruptly, taking his seat.

"Excuse me?" My train of thought has now been entirely derailed.

"That was what you were wondering, wasn't it?"

I cock my head to one side, studying him. "Why?"

"Oh, I have my reasons right here." He tugs the corner of a piece of paper from his pocket.

"What is it?"

Chandler gulps down his coffee like he's taking a shot. "It's a message from a friend, containing information about my future—or what will be my future if I go back. Frankly, I don't like how things turn out, so I'm staying here instead."

"You can't do that. It's against the Rules."

"I'm pretty sure I've broken every time travel rule and probably created a dozen paradoxes, but what can I say?" He shrugs nonchalantly, as if destroying the time-space continuum were only as reproachable as breaking his grandma's favorite vase. "Here, I can start over, make a new life for myself, and enjoy myself a bit. Plus, the Punch-In is excellent."

"Punch-In?"

"Yup. Punch-In is one of my favorite things about the future. Restaurants send out electronically coded menus, so whenever you want to order something, you just punch the buttons. Bam, it shows up on your doorstep ten minutes later. It's like take-out, but a million times better."

That makes me laugh despite myself. Of all the things in this amazing future, the improvements to *take-out* are what impress him the most. Figures.

"I suppose once you get over the disappointment that a hundred years into the future, they still haven't manufactured flying cars, an improved method of takeout might seem pretty exciting," I say.

"Well of course they don't have flying cars *here*." Before I can figure out if he's joking, he continues. "The point is, I don't want to live in a world where I already know my own future, or the world's future. It's boring knowing how everything turns out."

"So this is, what, some sort of existential crisis?"

"Something like that." He looks over my shoulder, an unreadable expression on his face. "Of course, maybe it's all inevitable anyway. You PITTA Retrievers know quite a bit about time travel, right?"

I nod. The strap of my watch suddenly seems too tight. I twist it around on my wrist.

"You tell me. How many times have you changed the past? Or your clients—how many times have they really, truly done something to alter history? Killed their own grandmother, or whatever?" His joking demeanor has taken a sudden, serious tone that makes me nervous. "Is it even possible?"

"We try *not* to change the past. We don't know *how* it might affect things. That's why the Rules are in place. We take them very seriously and insist our clients do as well. They're a safeguard, in case something like the Butterfly Effect or paradoxes or chaos theory actually do exist, you know?"

"That's exactly the kind of thing I'm talking about. How often have things like that happened in the time you've been at PITTA?"

The question makes me pause. My entire job revolves around making sure the Rules are followed, and our pre-Jump screening usually does a decent job of weeding out anyone who intends to purposely break them. My mind fixates on my last Retrieval—could our interference in 1912 have changed the past?

"I think that even if the past can change," I say with a slight tremble in my voice, "it would have to be an incredibly large action to create an incredibly large effect in our time. Maybe our clients are making small, insignificant changes, but if they are, history would find some way of explaining the discrepancies in a logical way."

"What do you mean?"

I search my memories for an example. Only one comes to mind.

"Like *The Wreck of the Titan.*"

"Which is?"

"A book." I roll my eyes, but seeing the serious look on Chandler's face, quickly avert my gaze back to the holographic green logo on my coffee cup. "A man named Morgan Robertson wrote *Futility: The Wreck of the Titan,* a novella about an 'unsinkable' ocean liner that, one April, hits an iceberg in the North Atlantic and—due to an insufficient number of lifeboats—causes the death of over half of its 2500 passengers."

"Sounds like a *Titanic* rip-off."

"Exactly. But *Futility* was published fourteen years before the *Titanic* sank."

Chandler lets out a low whistle. "So you think the author was a traveler, like us?"

"Not necessarily. But it's possible that one of our clients met up with him or someone he knew and the story was told before it was supposed to be. It's not like it changed anything, though. It's not as if the White Star Line read Robertson's story and thought 'oh, boy, we'd better make sure to have enough life boats!'"

"So then, why all the Rules? If it doesn't matter anyway?"

"I told you, the Rules are a safeguard. In that particular case, the result might've been a strangely prophetic book. No big deal. But who's to say next time it won't make a difference? We need the Rules to prevent major changes from taking place."

"You sure are stuck on those Rules, aren't you?" He grins. "I'll bet you were a teacher's pet in grade school, weren't you?"

"What does that—?"

"Regardless," he says, interrupting my protest. "I've seen my future. I looked into the crystal ball, so to speak, and I know what happens, at least if your theory about things being unchangeable is true. And I don't like it. It's like reading the last chapter of a book first. I don't want to know how it ends."

I don't necessarily disagree with anything he's said, but still, it's my job to bring him back. And if Dr. Wells is right, my life is on the line here, too, and that's far more important than some silly, philosophical misgivings.

"Wait a minute," I say, suddenly realizing what he's said. "What do you mean, my 'theory about things being unchangeable'? Haven't you been in dozens of possible futures? Isn't that the point of TUB's research; that things *are* changeable? They said they need to determine which choices will create the best possible outcomes. Why are you so concerned about what happens to you in just one of the timelines if there's an infinite number to choose from?"

Chandler chuckles, a quiet laugh at the back of his throat. His hands tear at the disposable coffee cup, shredding the biodegradable material into slivers. I purse my lips and glare at him.

"What?" I ask.

"That's what they told you, huh?"

I nod, narrowing my eyes in suspicion.

"My guess is that they were trying to instill confidence in you. Either that, or they were just being their typical lying selves."

"What do you mean?"

"We're not exactly as experienced as they'd have you believe. We've only Jumped to the future three times, each instance to investigate a particular project that—in our era—is still top secret."

"The *Continuum*?" I guess.

He nods, making a pyramid with the slivers of paper left over from his cup. "My first trip was short, only a few days. I checked on the status of the *Continuum*'s progress and its exact location in space, then Extracted back. A few months later, I Jumped out here. In December, I made a quick trip back to report to TUB, and after that I decided to stay here. I haven't seen enough of the future to know if it's alterable because so far everything's played out just as TUB anticipated."

"Butcher and Baker haven't Jumped forward to any other points in time, either?"

He scoffs. "Butcher and Baker are cowards; neither of them would dare set foot in a DeLorean Box."

I hold my head in my hands, cursing myself for missing what now seems so obvious. I can't believe I so drastically misread the situation. For a fleeting moment, I entertain the idea that Chandler might be lying but quickly dismiss it. The whole time I was at TUB, I could tell they were hiding something, that they were untrustworthy and just using me. Chandler, on the other hand, has been upfront and honest, at least as far as I can tell from his body language. Plus, his story makes more sense.

"They told me you were researching an immigration issue." I'm still in shock that I was so easily fooled.

"Immigration, *emigration*..." He shrugs, as if it's just a matter of semantics. "Technically, we're citizens of the *Continuum* now, not the United States. They had to set up their own Governing Committee, since the people here are from all over the world. So, yeah, I guess you could say it's an immigration issue. TUB's pretty skilled at spouting half-truths. They probably just didn't want you to chicken out."

I start to object, but he puts up a finger to interject.

"By the way, that's yet another phrase you probably shouldn't use. Chickens in 2112 are apparently large and vicious, thanks to corporations pumping them full of hormones all those years. Calling someone a 'chicken' has *quite* a different meaning now."

He brushes the paper-pyramid off the table into his hand, checks his watch, and stands up. "So, that's my story. You can go back and tell TUB it doesn't matter how many Retrievers they send, I'm not going back. Now if you'll excuse me, I have somewhere I need to be."

My mind is still boggled, trying to wrap itself around my recent discoveries. Chandler is at the door before I snap out of it.

"I can't go back," I call, but he's already pushed through the revolving doors. His blonde head disappears into the crowd, and I throw down my napkin, muttering, "Not without you."

CHAPTER FOURTEEN: APRIL 13, 2112

I feel like kicking myself for letting Chandler push me around. It's my job to bring him back to the present—no ifs, ands, or buts about it.

Bolting upright so fast I nearly knock over my chair, I push my coffee cup into a recycling receptacle and dash out the door. It takes a moment for my PVD to adjust to the light again, and I scan the street, looking for Chandler's blonde mop of hair. I spot him about a block away and follow at a cautious distance as he expertly navigates the city streets.

As I round a block, the noise intensifies, and suddenly I'm one of the tallest people in the crowd. A wave of children pour out of a large building, pushing and shoving one another as they bustle out into the world. Blue letters above the door spell out "SCHOOL," and all around are the gleeful shouts of students recently released from their studies.

"See you tomorrow!"

"Are you still coming over on Friday?"

"Aw, zap it, I have a ton of homework!"

The tidal wave of small, excitable bodies nearly pushes me backwards, but I step to one side and scan the tops of the bobbing heads.

When I spot him, I'm dumbstruck.

Chandler crouches to hug a small, thin boy with dark hair who looks about eight years old. The two share a short conversation, and they both break out into laughter. Then Chandler grasps the child's hand and adjusts the shoulder strap on his bag. Their arms swing together, and the boy continues jabbering excitedly. They disappear into the crowd, and by the time I catch my breath, I have no idea where to even start looking for them again.

What just happened here? How does Chandler know this kid, this young boy from the future?

I bite my lip, trying to plan my next move. I need more information. Time to head back to the library.

With the help of Myah the Disgruntled Librarian, I download a map of the *Continuum*, as well as a photo directory of all of its citizens, and settle in for a long afternoon of flipping through thousands of entries.

I skim the photographs of the citizens, people of all races, with ages ranging from one to sixty-two. I must have been looking through them for at least an hour when I nearly flip past the picture of the thin, dark-haired boy labeled "DODGE GREENLEY."

It's him. The boy. He has a lopsided smile and dimples, and there's a sparkle in his eyes that makes him look mischievous. Below Dodge Greenley's name is an address: Apartment Y, Number 403.

Bingo.

As I pull out my notebook to write down the address, I hear a rich baritone voice behind me that sounds strangely familiar.

"I was wondering if you might show me how to scan a copy of these blueprints?"

Myah sighs. "Our copier is this way, Mr.—"

"Please, call me Allen. And thank you for your help. You've been very kind."

Allen? Marie had called her fiancé Allen, though why that thought jumps into my mind now, I don't know. Maybe because this man has a thick British accent and a formal manner of speech just like his.

I lean in my chair, trying to catch the man's reflection in the dark computer screen as he follows Myah to another room. When I see him, I nearly fall off the seat.

From the split-second glimpse I get of him, it looks like the same man. Of course it can't be. It's not possible. My mind works dizzily, trying to rationalize his apparent appearance here. Maybe I'm just being paranoid? Maybe my suppressed guilt over the botched Retrieval is making me hear things, like in Poe's *Tell-Tale Heart*?

For five, ten minutes maybe, I sit silently, my ears straining for his voice, my eyes fixed on the reflections in the screen. When he emerges from the other room with a stack of papers and slides out the revolving door, I jump from my chair and follow. His shadow disappears to the left. Slowly, I step out into the brilliant "outdoors."

The man standing on the sidewalk, now in profile, leans down to scribble something in his leather-bound notebook. Even from here, I can see the silver compass on the cover, which looks exactly the same as the last time I saw it. The man himself looks different—older, thinner, and wearier—but the dark mustache and ample eyebrows leave no doubt to his identity. I press myself against the wall, praying he hasn't noticed me, or if he has, that he won't recognize me from the Southampton dock where I stole away his fiancée.

How can this be? What is a man from 1912 doing on a space colony two hundred years into his future? I have no idea how he ended up here, but I need to find out. It can't be a coincidence that we're both here, now.

When I look again, he's gone. Part of me is relieved. I'm not even sure if I should be pursuing or fleeing from him.

The lighting panels have dimmed, and slowly the crowds are

dispersing. I should go back inside the library or find somewhere to stay the night, but the longer I stand there, staring down the road, the more apparent it is that I will *not* be able to get a wink of sleep. Somewhere out there, a mysterious traveler from the past may be searching for me, maybe even plotting revenge against me for something that happened two hundred years ago. My imagination runs amok, and I picture him standing over my bed, brandishing his journal in one hand and a dagger in the other.

"That's crazy," I say aloud. But now that the image has introduced itself into my head, I can't shake it. I also can't stay here in the street, and there's only one other place I can think to go.

I re-read the paper in my hand. Time to pay Chandler a surprise visit.

CHAPTER FIFTEEN: APRIL 13, 2112

I jab at every tiny button and dial on my PVD, trying to find the map I'd downloaded at the library. It takes me an embarrassingly long time to pull it up, but when I do, I mentally applaud myself for conquering this strange, future technology.

On the holographic map in the corner of my glasses, I locate the housing community on the outskirts of the city, where the urban area ends and the agricultural fields begin. My brisk pace brings me in view of these buildings within a few minutes. Each building is around fifteen stories high; with the reflective glass paneling over its entire surface, I can't tell for sure.

Even as the time approaches 9pm, people mingle on the grassy areas between the buildings, arriving home from work, greeting neighbors, and simply *living*. In my travels, one of the things I enjoy most is seeing the everyday lives of normal, ordinary people; it helps me remember what I used to be like, before I met Dr. Wells and my life became entirely *un*-ordinary.

Obviously this part of the community was carefully planned, much like the commercial areas' color coordination. Each building, though constructed identically—at least as far as I can tell—seems to have its own personality and identity. The further I wander into the development, the more apparent this becomes.

The apartments in the first row remind me of frat houses. The young men and women who gather on the lawn and recline on the picnic tables are noisy, excitable, and don't seem to care that it's nighttime. The glass surfaces of the bottom floors are smeared with window paint displaying names and symbols. Some I recognize as international sports teams' logos, but others are unfamiliar—perhaps too new.

Passing the next row feels like stepping into a completely new neighborhood, a new *world*. It's almost as if the buildings themselves pulled one too many all-nighters, finally got real jobs, and grew up. The buildings and lawns are impeccable—neat, tidy, and clean, without a smudge on the glass or a scrap of paper in the yard. A few couples snuggle on benches under trees whose leaves are too silky and flawless to be real. A group of 20-somethings play a card game around a patio table. I keep my head low and avoid eye contact, and they don't even seem to notice me pass.

Down the next row, the sounds of the first block's revelers already seem distant and indistinct. These buildings are quiet, though they show signs of active daytime life. Play structures, riding toys, and wagons are scattered in the green spaces. One corner even houses a pool with a slide, but it seems bedtime has already reached these apartments.

The fourth row is quieter still, though there are a few people hovering outside the buildings, chatting in low voices. Here, the windows are dark, as if the residents are either out or asleep. The lawns lack children's toys, but there are plenty of tennis courts, swimming pools, and even a driving range.

I'm intrigued by the novelty of grouping together residents by their respective stages of life—isn't that normally how people choose to organize themselves anyway?

The last apartments are quietest and darkest, farthest from the city and closest to the vast fields that stretch on to the horizon—well, the artificial horizon, where the curved panes of glass meet the ground. On the lawn of Apartment Y, a collection of gnomes hide among artificial topiaries, and a gray-haired man rocks on a free-standing porch swing, reading a thick book. I brush my fingers over a collection of idle wind chimes as I approach the door, setting off a soft tinkling of music in the otherwise still, quiet air.

I push my way through the revolving door and ring the bell for number 403. Chandler's face pops up on the screen.

"Why are you living among the elderly?" I ask, instead of the question I meant to voice, which was "Can we talk?"

A grin spreads across his face. "I'll buzz you in."

The potpourri and ointment smell of Chandler's apartment wafts out into the hallway. The door is open, so I enter cautiously, unnerved by the embroidered doilies on his end tables and cat figurines frozen in mid-scamper in shadow boxes on his wall. Matching recliners rest in the center of the room. In the corner stands a bookshelf that's home to stacks of old crocheting catalogs, *Better Homes and Gardens* magazines, and a handful of books with titles like *Living in Space for Dummies* and *What Your Travel Agent Won't Tell You About Space Travel*. Since I personally have never had much interest in crocheting, I'm about to dismiss the contents of the shelf when I spot an old-fashioned, leather-bound journal perched atop a stack of yellowing *Popular Astronautics* from 2080.

A silver compass is embossed on the cover.

The voice from the library rings in my ears as I reach for the journal. It can't be a coincidence.

My fingers are about to close on the dark binding when I hear a throat cleared behind me. I spin away, feeling as guilty as a child caught poking his finger into his sibling's birthday cake.

"I didn't hear you."

"No worries." Chandler waves a hand. "I'm not one to talk; it's not my stuff, either."

"Really?" I hold up a copy of *Crock Pot Cooking in Space.* "This isn't yours?"

"Ha, no. Though the recipe for stroganoff isn't half bad." He peers at the shelf and—reaching around me—picks up the journal. "Is this what you were looking at?"

"No."

He tips his head. "I thought we were past the lies."

I sigh. "Where did you get it?"

"You know whose it is, don't you?"

I squeeze my lips shut. What does he know about Allen?

Chandler dangles the journal in front of my face, then slaps it down into his palm. The pages fan out to reveal empty sheets of paper. He tosses it to me, and I catch it.

"I only know one person with a journal like this one," I say, "but he's not supposed to be here."

"Wait." For the first time all day, Chandler looks surprised. "You're telling me Journal Guy isn't a Retriever?"

"No, he's not a Retriever. He's not even from our present."

"Huh." Chandler drops into an armchair. "I assumed he was another PITTA guy and that you were working together. Here I figured he was just a bit incompetent."

"What do you mean?"

"I was standing right in front of him, so if he was here to Retrieve me, he was doing a terrible job tracking me down."

"You've seen him? When?" My pulse quickens.

Chandler eyes me suspiciously. "Recently. You swear you're not working with him?"

"I swear."

"Well, then, maybe we can help one another out here, because I have to admit, my own methods of investigation have thus far come up short."

"Your methods of investigation?"

"Wait. Is this really what you came down here to discuss? Or are you going to try to convince me to go back again? Because that's not going to work."

I automatically start compiling a list of all the reasons he should go back: his job with TUB, my job at PITTA, TUB's threats on my life, not to mention a little thing known as the time-space continuum…

"No," I say, interrupting my own thoughts. I have a whole week to convince Chandler to Extract, and if we're working together, maybe I can gain his trust. Then maybe I'll be able to find out what the message is that convinced him to stay and maybe find some way to convince him otherwise. It's a lot of maybes, but often in my job, a little patience pays off.

"I think there's more at stake here than just my mission." I choose my words very carefully as I explain my trip to 1912 and how Allen witnessed his fiancée's Extraction.

"If my actions in the past have resulted in his presence here, I'm the one responsible to make it right. I *need* to figure out why he's here. I think he might be following me."

"Possible," Chandler says, "but it still doesn't all fit. I've been trailing this guy for a week already, and you just got here."

"You've been trailing him? How did you find him?"

"Same way I found you."

"What do you mean?" I *knew* the meeting at the library couldn't have been a coincidence.

Chandler motions to one of the recliners. I perch on the edge of the cushion and eye the floral upholstery while he settles into the other chair. He looks as if he's trying to determine how to best answer me, but I interrupt.

"Why are you living here?"

"Huh?"

"Whose home is this?" I gesture to the floral wallpaper, the doilies, the cookbooks.

"What, you don't like my throw pillows?"

I scowl. Chandler grins.

"The apartment belonged to a lovely old lady by the name of Hannah Greenley, who passed away from natural causes shortly after I arrived. I've been telling the other residents that I'm her estranged son, though in reality, I just altered the record in the housing database—"

"The housing database?"

"Ah, one of the many fabulous features of the Governing Committee's Grid. The housing database keeps track of who's assigned to which building."

"And you have access to that?"

"Not *technically*. Let's just say I have a way with computers, hmm?" The twinkle in his eye tells me that his 'way with computers' might not be entirely legal. "It was the reason TUB hired me."

"So you're a hacker?"

"You could call it that."

"And how illegal is that, exactly?" I narrow my eyes.

"How legal is any of this? How legal is your little travel agency? How legal is my reconnaissance here?"

I open my mouth to protest when his words sink in. "What? Then TUB isn't a government agency?"

Chandler's eyebrows jerk up so high they're nearly buried underneath his hair. "Government? Really? That's what they told you? Wow. I knew they were brassy, but they've really stepped it up."

My mouth opens and shuts, but no words come out.

"No," he says. "TUB has nothing to do with the government, except that they have deep pockets as well as other, less *polite* ways of getting the government—and others—to do what they want. How did you think a project like the *Continuum* got pushed through?"

"What's their interest in the *Continuum*?" It may be a stupid question, but I need to hear the answer.

"You really don't know? TUB *is* the *Continuum*, in its infancy.

They're the ones planning it, planting the seeds in the minds of politicians and CEOs and investors, getting everyone on board, and getting all the major players in their back pockets so they can be the ones to benefit when the money starts rolling in.

"I was interested in the project because I wanted to explore the possibility of space habitation. Maybe I'm a romantic, but it sounded like a way to make a difference in the world. Or *off* it, I suppose. The others, well...I found out they were just in it for the money. A project that takes over ninety years to complete is a great way to guarantee job security, especially if you have the technology to verify it's not going to go bottoms-up halfway through."

"Which is where you came in."

"Risk management. Believe me, if my first Jump showed the project was a flop, there's no way they'd have stuck with it; they'd have turned their scheming to other pursuits. But, as it turned out, the *Continuum* actually did succeed, so they got the distinction of being the spearheads."

"And you? I suppose they'll set you up nicely as well when you get back."

"Fat chance. Besides, does it look like I care about money? I mean, look at our apartment. Does it seem like money's a major priority?" He gestures around to the quaint, doily-adorned dwelling.

"You said 'our.'"

"Huh?"

"'Look at our apartment.' Who else lives here, Chandler?" My voice sounds shrill and accusing.

Our stare-off is intense, but I must be the winner, because he finally sighs and gives in. "Dodge."

"Dodge? Is that a dog?" I wonder if he knows that I already know, that I'm only asking to test his integrity.

He scrunches up his face. "Have you seen pets of any variety—any animals at all, for that matter—aboard the *Continuum*? Of course he's not a dog. He's a kid. He's a bit of a menace, but overall a good kid."

"Does he not have any parents? What is he doing here? Why are you involving yourself in the life of a little boy? You know, it's one thing for a client to get caught up in things and form relationships with people from other eras, but you're a professional. What were you thinking? That is in direct violation of Rule #8." The sharp tone rises again, and I force myself to take a few deep breaths to calm down.

"Look," he says, "I'd just Jumped here and went out to get some groceries. The little punk tried to swipe some food from my bag, and I caught him at it. I offered to take him home to his parents, but he claimed he didn't have any. Instead of turning him over to the Governing Committee and having to explain who I am and why my name isn't on the *Continuum*'s manifest, I sat him down to see if we could come to some sort of arrangement."

"I thought the *Continuum*'s residents were all single adults or family units; how did a kid end up here without anyone to go home to?"

"That's what I wondered, too. Turned out, he lived with his grandmother."

"The owner of this apartment."

"Exactly. She was one of the older residents of the *Continuum*, and though the doctors predicted that she'd live for at least another sixty years, she had some sort of freak heart attack and died. Dodge hadn't told anyone yet, for fear that they'd send him back to Earth the next time one of the bigwig diplomat shuttles came around. Apparently, he doesn't have any other living relatives, so he'd be sent off to a Home for Superfluous Children. Doesn't *that* sound like a welcoming place?"

I ignore the challenge in his set jaw, the unspoken question of what I would have done in the same situation, and stick with the facts.

"So he needed a legal guardian, and you needed a place to stay?"

"That pretty much sums it up. I hacked into the system and

designated myself his uncle. Then, when he reported his grandmother's death, custody passed to me. He teaches me all about the twenty-second century, and I bring home the bacon. Not literally, though. Bacon's become a precious commodity since the mad pig disease of 2092, or at least that's what Dodge—"

"Spare me the history lesson. How old is he?"

"Seven."

"Seriously?" I rise to my feet. My muscles are too tense; they need to move. "You brought a seven-year-old kid into this?"

"Elise." He leans forward, his face now serious. "He needed someone and I happened to be there. Seven-year-olds can't make it on their own. He may be smart, but he's just a kid."

The thought makes me uneasy; I can't deny his heart was in the right place, even if what he did was stupid. Some unfamiliar maternal part of my heart tugs within me for the poor boy. What's going to happen to him when Chandler returns to the present?

Chandler sits back and crosses his arms.

I throw my hands up in defeat. "I don't have time to deal with this; we'll discuss it later. For now, just tell me how you found Allen and why you have a journal that looks like his."

"Believe it or not, I have a brilliant plan."

CHAPTER SIXTEEN: APRIL 13, 2112

"You plan to swap it out?" I ask. A blank journal that looks like Allen's makes Chandler's "brilliant" plan somewhat obvious.

"Exactly. See, I discovered he was on the *Continuum* about a week ago." He jumps to his feet and says, "Screen on."

The blank wall on the other side of the room lights up, revealing a screen like the ones at the library, only much larger. With a few finger flicks, Chandler manipulates the displayed images, too quickly for me to comprehend. I stop watching the screen and look at him instead. His wrists snap and his fingers fly. He pushes his lip out to one side in concentration. Then he stops.

"What did you do?"

He grins. "I just hacked into the Governing Committee's Grid and pulled up the day's retina scan records."

Sure enough, floating off the wall in three dizzying dimensions, are lists and files and folders. I approach the wall cautiously and reach out a single finger. When it connects with one of the files, I can almost *feel* it on my skin, resisting slightly as I tug it open, a gift-wrapped box of digital information hovering in the air above me.

"This is incredible."

"The output may look complex, but once you figure out the

system, it's not that much different than the quantum computers being developed back in the twenty-first century. The Grid was designed for maximum efficiency, so once you have a feel for it, you can find nearly anything. I wanted to keep an eye out for anyone who might be coming to Retrieve me. With the information on the Grid, I can determine what anyone on the *Continuum* is doing at any given time by tracking their retina scans."

"So how'd you find Allen?"

"When I first arrived, I discovered a glitch in the system. See, the *Continuum*'s network only has its residents' retina scans on file. They don't pull from the worldwide database because, well, they don't have to. The only people who travel back and forth are political diplomats, so anytime a new scan shows up, it automatically gets logged into the system as a 'Diplomat Guest'. The Governing Committee's system doesn't even ping it out unless the same scan continues getting hits after a week—the maximum length of time diplomats are allowed on the colony—so I've got a notification set up to tell me immediately if a new 'Diplomat Guest' scan goes through. Then I manually check it out myself."

"What about yours? You're not registered here."

"Added myself to the system. So when this guy's scans showed up and I knew no diplomats had arrived recently, I started following him because, like you, I thought he might be a threat to my mission. Or, a threat to me *avoiding* my mission, I guess."

"What made you think he was with PITTA?"

"I wasn't sure initially, but then I saw he had one of these babies." He reaches onto the top bookshelf and pulls out a shiny black sphere.

My breath catches. "A Wormhole."

Seeing the device in Chandler's hand tempts me. I could stop him right there and force his thumb onto the button, propelling him abruptly back to 2012 where he belongs. Well, where he's *from*, anyway, I think and then mentally scold myself for that concession. Of course he belongs in 2012. That's where he originated, and that's where his life is. Everyone must return to his own time. There's a reason it's Rule #1.

Chandler sees me staring and stuffs his Wormhole into his pocket. I'm about to wonder aloud where Allen might have gotten one, when it hits me: Marie's original device, the one she left back in 1912. In the chaos following her Retrieval, I'd never gotten a chance to report it missing. Another error on my part, though, in my defense, I hadn't exactly expected to be kidnapped that afternoon.

"What's he been doing?" I ask.

"Raiding supply closets, breaking into surveillance rooms, studying blueprints—"

"Blueprints. That's what he was looking at when I saw him at the library."

"Oh, and he spends a lot of time watching old vids of some pop star. You know, the one who did that song that goes '*Nah nah nah nah na—*"

"I know the one." Marie.

"Here's what I don't get." I pace the room. "Our DeLorean Box isn't even capable of sending someone forward in time, so how did he get here?"

"Not TUB's Box; you've seen how secure theirs is. Besides, his Wormhole isn't the same."

"What?"

"It's got multiple buttons and dials." He reaches toward his pocket, as if to pull out his as a visual aide, but then thinks better of it and turns to the screen instead, zooming in on an image of Allen sitting on a park bench. "See?"

The device in Allen's hands is definitely a Wormhole, but at the same time, it's not. I step closer until I'm enveloped in the holographic image, the 3D projection of the Wormhole-Device-that's-not-a-Wormhole-Device hovering in the air within my grasp.

"It's similar…" I squint to get a better look. "But it's like he gave it upgrades. I wonder what it does."

"Seems pretty obvious to me." Chandler shrugs. "It does the same things as ours, but better."

CHAPTER SEVENTEEN: APRIL 14, 2112

Allen

Allen stepped off the early morning solar train and patted his pocket, ensuring that his precious 'time sphere' was there. It was a nervous tic, an action he caught himself doing more and more frequently nowadays. He removed his journal from his opposite pocket and scribbled furiously with the tiny stub of pencil he always carried with him, recalculating to be certain his numbers were correct, that today was truly the day he'd come here to observe. His one chance to ensure everything was in place.

The "sky" here was useless here for determining his location, so he was forced to don a set of those infernal spectacles. His finger hovered over the button that would show him her image and fill his head with her voice. No, there wasn't time for nostalgia today. After double-checking his bearings, he set off at a jaunty pace. As he walked, he reviewed his mental checklist.

Acquire provisions and shelter. Test retina scan. Check documented time table. Plan emergency escape. Acquire emergency supplies: oxygen tanks, suits, food, water. Determine ideal location for viewing area. He stopped mid-stride.

A surveillance room, perhaps, he thought, and pulled out his notebook again to make a note. Watching from afar would be ideal, though he wondered if potential clients might think that too far removed.

He sighed, returning his journal to its proper place, then pulling it out again to check his figures. It seemed to be all he did nowadays—check and recheck, for it was only in those numbers and figures and calculations, in this planning and organizing, that he could lose himself, could forget all he'd lost.

After Marie, he hadn't known what to do with himself. And perhaps this most recent venture of his was just a distraction to keep his mind from returning to her. To keep himself from clicking the dials and pushing the button that would bring him back to her time. Perhaps part of him hoped that it would lead her to him. He suspected all these things may be true, at least in part, but never allowed himself to dwell on it.

The outer, domed surface of the space colony curved gently upward, meeting with brilliantly lit panels that made spots appear in his vision. He closed his eyes and soaked in the heat. Adrenaline pumped through his body at the knowledge of what would occur here in a mere matter of hours. He pulled out the pencil and began his calculations again.

CHAPTER EIGHTEEN: APRIL 14, 2112

I don't know what time it is when I finally wake. With the unnerving lack of shadows outside, the day is perpetually stuck on noontime from very first moment the panels brighten in the morning. Nor do I remember where I am, until I see that I'm still in that awful, shapeless suit. Right. Chandler's apartment. I have five days left to complete this Extraction, and now another man from another time to deal with, too.

Chandler and I spent hours the night before formulating plans and hypotheses, but we didn't get any closer to discovering why Allen is here, how he altered the Wormhole, or what we should do about it. Nor did I get any closer to convincing Chandler to Extract back to our present. When I started to doze standing up, Chandler offered me the privacy of the master bedroom while he crashed in the living room recliner.

Awake now, I stumble into the kitchen, and Chandler greets me with a smile and a cup of coffee.

"Here's another thing I love about this place." Chandler hands me the steaming drink. "They've figured out how to insulate cups so that coffee doesn't lose its heat or flavor. That cup's been sitting out for hours already and I can guarantee it'll be as fresh and toasty as if it'd just been brewed."

I take a sip and have to agree that there's something miraculous about it. I turn to sit in the armchair I occupied last night, but it's already taken. The same scrawny, dark-haired kid I saw at the school stares at me with wide eyes.

"Who are you?" he asks.

"I—I'm Elise." I put out a hand in greeting, but he just frowns at it. Chandler steps in.

"Ah, no one's really used handshakes since the so-called 'Dragon Flu' of the 2030s," he explains. "Dodge, this is Elise. We work together."

Dodge watches me with an open curiosity that makes me want to sink into the floor.

"I'm going to grab a fresh suit and hit the shower before we head out," Chandler says, oblivious to my discomfort. "Make yourself at home."

"Are you a spy, too?" Dodge asks as soon as Chandler's gone. His huge eyes have grown even wider. I feel like a bug under a microscope.

"Um...yeah." I add that to my mental tally of half-truths.

"Do you like basketball?"

"Um, sort of. It's been awhile since I've played."

"I have a game tomorrow. You can come if you want. There's always extra seats, and Uncle Chandler won't mind sitting next to you. He doesn't have many friends here." He says this last part in a hushed, conspiratorial tone. I'm not sure how to take it, so I just tap my coffee mug and nod.

"It's because of his job," Dodge says matter-of-factly. "He has a lot of secrets."

I nod again. We scrutinize each other silently for a minute or two. I have no idea what sort of things seven-year-old boys like to talk about, especially not in 2112, so I say the first thing that pops into my head. "I know he's not really your uncle."

Dodge's eyebrows shoot upward, but then he shrugs as if it's not a big deal after all. "He adopted me. I'm glad he did. I didn't want to go back and end up at one of those Superf— Superfloat—one of those Children's Homes."

"They're pretty bad?"

He nods gravely. "My friend Bo said his cousin knew someone who got sent to one. He said they were always sad and they got sick a lot and they never got to eat desserts or play sports or listen to music or get birthday presents or *anything*."

"Sounds awful."

"It is," he says matter-of-factly. "Plus, I like Uncle Chandler. He does his spy stuff while I'm at school so that when I'm home we can hang out."

"Oh, yeah? What sort of things do you do together?"

"Sometimes we play basketball at the park, and we play virtual games together, too. He helps me with my homework, and lately he's been trying to teach me how to cook. We tried making a stir fry the other day, but he burnt it. It had smoke coming out and everything." He makes big, *whooshing* gestures and a sound like an explosion. I can't help but laugh.

"We've been making good use of Grandmother Greenley's cookbooks," Chandler says, entering from the other room. He smiles at me, and Dodge's gaze flits back and forth between us.

"Are you two in negotiations?" Dodge asks, wrinkling up his nose. I turn to Chandler for an explanation.

"No, we're most certainly *not* in negotiations," Chandler says. "Have you de-plaqued your teeth this morning?"

Dodge scowls but hops off the chair and hurries off to the bathroom.

"Negotiations?" I ask once he's out of earshot.

"Dating," Chandler says, clearing the dishes off the counter and dumping them through a hole in the wall. "When the United States' divorce rate hit 90% back in the 2070s, states started requiring couples to draw up prenuptial agreements before they could obtain a marriage license. The media joked that the government was turning dating into a series of negotiations, and the term kind of stuck."

Dodge rushes in and runs up to Chandler. He grins widely, proudly displaying his newly de-plaqued teeth for Chandler's inspection.

"Nice job." Chandler nods. "Elise and I have some work to do this afternoon, so I'm going to drop you off next door at Mrs. Finney's. She can help you with your homework, and if I'm not back by bedtime you can crash in her guest room. I've already asked."

"Aww, do I have to?"

"Sure do. Bring your PVD so I can get a hold of you if I need to." Dodge scrambles off toward a back room, presumably to grab his glasses.

"Really? That well-behaved little boy is the 'menace' who tried to steal your groceries?"

Chandler grins. "He's a sweet kid. So, you ready to hunt down a rogue time traveler? Looks like he already made his first transaction today: one ticket on the solar train."

"Solar train?"

Chandler pulls up a map of the *Continuum* and focuses in on the upper surface, turning it so that we're viewing it from above. From the aerial perspective, it looks like a perfect circle with a square inscribed within it and a smaller square centered within that.

"The small, inner square is the city itself. Everyone on the *Continuum* lives in the housing community, here. Most people walk or ride saucers to work, but farmers, engineers, and the military personnel commute on the solar train. It travels from the city's edge, through the agricultural fields, then around through the three engineering zones to the Control Center."

He gestures as he talks, his finger finally landing inside the holographic control center, a dark sliver wedged between agricultural fields and the circle's outer rim.

"Do you think that's where he's going? To the Control Center?" I try to keep the panic from my voice.

"I thought so, but apparently not. See, they only charged him for one unit, which means if he boarded anywhere within the city, the first stop would be where the agricultural fields meet Engineering Sector 2."

"And what's out there?"

"Agricultural fields. Engineering Sector 2."

I roll my eyes. "Seriously."

"Nothing else of interest."

"You don't think he could be sabotaging the colony, do you?"

"Stealing supplies, breaking into secure areas... I suppose that would make sense. But why?" Chandler shakes his head. "Besides, the most essential life support equipment—water tanks, oxygen tanks, artificial gravity generators—are all underground, so to speak, in the lower levels. There might be access to those levels from Sector 2, but there are more convenient elevators in the city, if that was his goal. The only things in Sector 2 are the launch bays for incoming space craft, a bunch of warehouses, and...huh."

"What? What else is there?"

"The escape pods."

CHAPTER NINETEEN: APRIL 14, 2112

"What's the plan when we find Allen?" I ask once we're comfortably aboard the solar train, watching fields of corn whizzing by outside the chrome-framed windows.

"How do you normally operate?"

"I don't normally operate in situations like this." The way he turned the question around irritates me. "Most of my Extractions are people who desperately want to go back to their own time but can't because they've lost or broken their Wormholes. Though occasionally I'll get some highly emotional individual who's romanticized the past and can't bear the idea of returning and dealing with the messes they've left behind."

"Harsh."

"It's the truth. When someone tries to stay in the past, it generally isn't because they love it there so much; it's because they're running from something in their present."

The silence stretches on and the look in Chandler's eyes tells me I've inadvertently hit on something. I wasn't even thinking of him when I said it.

"What are you running from?" I ask.

The cold silence between us is broken by a voice in the tiny speakers of our personal glasses that announces our arrival at Sector 2—the same stop Allen disembarked at earlier today.

I glance out the window, curious to see what the engineers of the *Continuum* would stick all the way out here, miles from the city. It's a bit of a disappointment. Dozens of identical gray buildings of the same bland shape and construction rise up before us. Behind them, a row of larger buildings are positioned evenly along the curvature of the colony's edge. A solid band of white extends from the ground to a height just above the buildings where it meets the brilliant panels that seem blinding at this close range, even from behind my glasses.

"Now what?" I ask when we step onto the platform.

Chandler starts walking parallel to the buildings. "The launch bay with the escape pods is about two miles from here."

"What makes you think he's going for the escape pods?"

"Maybe he thinks he'll need a quick escape." Chandler squints toward the vacant, motionless city of concrete on our right and the sea of grain on our left. "He was on the *Titanic*, right? Maybe he wants to make sure there are enough lifeboats."

"Are there?"

Chandler shrugs. "Never thought to ask. Besides, what else would he want to see out here? This entire sector is a ghost town. Diplomats fly in occasionally, but most of these buildings are empty except for spare parts."

I fall behind, gazing out over the abandoned sector.

"You need a break already?"

"No, I'm fine," I say, though I have to jog to catch up. "Isn't it inconvenient to put the escape pods all the way out here?"

"Out of sight, out of mind. Everyone here signed on for fifty years, and the Governing Committee tries to ease that burden by not reminding the citizens too often of all they've left behind. If they have to pass escape pods every day on their way to work, someone having second thoughts about this whole thing might get the bright idea to steal one to return to Earth. So, they're tucked away in hopes that people forget they even exist."

Chandler spends the next twenty minutes or so rambling on about the mechanics of the escape pods, the supplies they carry, and how they've been programmed to automatically return to Earth's atmosphere and drop into the Pacific.

"In the launch bay," he says, "there are twenty-five giant glass tubes, lined up along the floor. The escape pods are kept inside, and in an emergency, the door slides open, the first pod is loaded up, and then the door shuts. A hydraulic mechanism pushes the other pods into it, creating enough pressure to launch it into space. Then the second pod gets loaded up, and the same thing happens to it. It's like one of those novelty pencils that were big back in the late '90s."

"Push-point pencils?"

"Sounds right. Anyway, each tube is assigned a letter that coordinates with—"

With one strong, swift motion, he pulls me backwards into the cornfield and clamps his hand over my mouth. I swing at him, trying to maneuver myself into a position where I have the advantage, but he presses an arm around me, immobilizing me, and whispers, "Stop fighting and look."

A man in a well-fitting suit is walking briskly between the buildings, approaching from the direction of the colony's outer edge. He walks purposefully, and from my vantage point, all I can see is the outline of his silhouette between the rows of gray buildings. It doesn't take much to imagine his dark outline twirling a mahogany cane and tipping a silk top hat.

CHAPTER TWENTY: APRIL 14, 2112

"There's no one around for miles." Chandler's whisper is full of excitement, but I just stare at him, uncomprehending. "This is our chance to see what's in that journal."

"What's your plan?"

Ignoring me, he dashes off, slinking between one building and the next. I watch in bewilderment as he creeps up on the oblivious Allen. They're moving out of my line of sight, so I follow the edge of the cornfield to keep up. What does Chandler have in mind? Should I be rushing forward to help him or sitting back and staying out of his way?

As Chandler closes the distance between them, I hurry my own pace, trying to stay low and out of sight. When he's only steps away, Chandler slows suddenly, and at a pace just faster than a jog, barrels right into Allen. His elbow jabs into Allen's side, and the two of them tumble to the ground along with the journal.

"Idiot!" I curse under my breath. That had to be the most un-subtle move I'd ever seen.

The dark silhouettes against the bright paneling are shadow puppets, all limbs and joints sticking out at awkward, unnatural angles as Chandler leans in to help Allen up. I crawl forward to get a better look.

The light fades like someone turning a dimmer switch, and I can make out their figures more clearly. I strain to hear the conversation and something flashes before my eyes. I blink, thinking it must be spots in my vision from staring toward the lighting panels for too long. But, no. It's on my PVD's lens. An icon flashes, and I flick the air in front of my face. Immediately, my left ear is bombarded by a familiar voice.

"—sorry! I was just out for a jog and didn't even see you there."

This was his plan?

"You know how it is," Chandler continues, "when you're looking directly into the panels. I can't believe there aren't more accidents out here with people being blinded by the lights."

"I am quite certain the agriculturists in this vicinity are accustomed to the panels," Allen says, his voice cool and even, "and I can't imagine *why* one would choose this particular area in which to exercise."

Allen brushes off his suit. He suddenly stops, pats his jacket, and then looks around frantically.

"Here." Chandler crouches to pick up the book. "You dropped this."

I hold my breath. Surely Allen noticed the swap.

For one glorious moment, it seems Chandler's gotten away with it. He turns and jogs toward me, throwing a friendly wave back in Allen's direction. One hand is tucked awkwardly in front of him; he must have hidden the journal beneath his shirt. Allen stands still and silent, holding the book Chandler gave him.

Come on, Chandler. Get out of there.

He's almost reached me when Allen opens the book. His whole body freezes and then quivers in anger. The next second, he's charging Chandler like an angry bear.

At the very moment Allen hits him from behind, Chandler whips his arm out and chucks the journal in my direction. Two shadows tussle, and this time the arms and legs are flying purposefully, thief and victim both caught up in the struggle. Fists connect with faces, accented by grunts and groans that make me flinch in sympathy.

My one advantage is that I haven't been spotted yet, but if I'm going to be any help to Chandler, I need to keep it that way. Both men are larger than me and obviously have experience in hand-to-hand combat. I know my strengths, and this kind of fight isn't one of them.

They break apart and circle one another.

"Who are you, and what do you want with my journal?"

"That's confidential," Chandler says. I wonder if he always has such a sarcastic sense of humor during his missions, or if he was more professional before going AWOL.

"You've been following me? A competitor, then?" Allen circles like a wolf.

"A competitor? What do you mean?"

There's a pause; Allen must be reconstructing his assumptions. "What do you want?"

"I want to know what you're doing here, instead of where you belong."

"Does anyone really belong here, on this chunk of metal floating in space?" Allen laughs at the concrete below them and the steel and glass panels above. "Do you really believe you belong here?"

"I belong here more than you do," Chandler says. "I know who you are."

"Which means you must know of my business as well. Tell me, then, what's your interest in my company?"

The circling stops and Chandler's fists drop slightly. In that split-second of hesitation, Allen draws back his elbow. With lightning speed, his fist smashes into his opponent's jaw.

I press my hand to my mouth to stifle a gasp as Chandler crumples to the ground. Allen kneels and pats down Chandler's clothes. When he stands, he's holding a handful of small objects which, at first, I can't place.

Then it hits me: Chandler's Wormhole Device. Broken into jagged bits in the fall.

Allen looks up. His head swivels from side to side as if he's searching for something. I slide deeper into the shadows.

He throws the pieces down and grinds them beneath his heel. Then he pulls out a handkerchief to dab the sweat from his brow. Replacing it, he consults his pocket watch, then curses and marches directly toward me.

I try making myself as small as possible, but he's not looking for me. He stops at the field's edge and conducts a scattered search for the journal, using his foot to push the loose dirt around. Dust hangs in the air, and I pray it provides enough cover to hide my movement. I crawl in the opposite direction, to where Chandler threw the journal, and snatch it up.

After a few final kicks, Allen curses again and runs his fingers through his hair. He strides back and stands over Chandler's fallen frame. With a scoff, he nudges the still form with his foot, then he leans in and heaves Chandler's body over one shoulder. Staggering, he turns and glances about before adjusting his burden and continuing his walk toward the *Continuum*'s escape pods.

The fields provide the best cover, so that's where I conceal myself. A stalk snaps underfoot, and the noise is deafening in the field's unnatural silence. Chandler mentioned there were no animals aboard the ship, but I hardly noticed until I got out here, where the air feels like a vacuum, devoid of birdcalls or chirping insects. Every footfall echoes, no matter how lightly I step.

I glance back and forth between Allen and the ground to avoid snapping any more stalks. He passes the launch bay containing the escape pods without even looking inside and continues walking until he reaches a small building. I'm nearly upon it before I can read the sign: "ELEVATOR."

Leaves whip my face as I follow him. He presses a button and the door opens with a noisy creak, making me suspect that this entrance is infrequently used. Once he steps inside, I'm left alone to consider my options. There are no numbers above the door to indicate where the lift stops, so any attempt to follow them would be blind. My PVD map shows over ten different underground levels beneath this part of the *Continuum*, each its own particular labyrinth of rooms, open areas, and hallways. I wouldn't even know where to start.

A half hour. I'll wait half an hour and then I'm going down whether Allen's returned or not. One way or another, I need Chandler. In the meantime, though, I need information. I sit cross-legged on the ground, positioning myself between two thick stalks so the elevator door is visible between them. It's time to see what secrets Allen's journal contains.

CHAPTER TWENTY-ONE: APRIL 14, 2112

My hand shakes as I slip Allen's journal out of my pocket and flip through it. To my irritation, the first half is full of mathematical equations and barely-legible notes, written in an unfamiliar shorthanded system. If it'd been in ancient Greek or Egyptian hieroglyphs, I could've translated it within an hour or two, but science is one language I've never mastered. With my limited knowledge of physics, I have no chance of deciphering his equations, either.

Finally, I find something familiar: a blueprint of Allen's souped-up Wormhole Device. It looks exactly like the image Chandler showed me. Each part is labeled, indicating the dials and switches that allow the traveler to choose the time and location of their Jump. Even Dr. Wells hasn't managed to make a portable device that will do this— that's why we have to use the big, bulky DeLorean box for our initial Jump—yet Allen has somehow managed to wedge the technology together, to create a hybrid that un-tethers him in time.

I study the sketches, feeling somewhat disloyal to Dr. Wells for my fascination with Allen's device, though it honestly is a superior design. Then I flip forward, hunting for any section that might contain more words than numbers. Something drops out from between the sheets and falls to the dirt.

It's an elaborately scripted letter, one addressed to *"My dearest Marie,"* which—due to the personal nature—I only skim. Allen describes his discovery of Marie's Wormhole, the days he spent tinkering with it to remove the thumbprint safeguard, and his final, courageous moments aboard the *Titanic* before the Wormhole whisked him into the future. It ends with the fervent promise:

I swear I will find you. Even if I must cross a dozen such oceans on a dozen beasts of the sea and defeat Poseidon, or break through the fabric of Time itself, I will do it. We will be together again, even if it takes a lifetime and costs me everything.

Something clatters, making me jump. The lift has returned to the surface, though the door's still shut. It must automatically return to this level. It's nearly been a half-hour, so I tuck the loose page into the journal and approach the elevator.

After pressing the button, I step aside so that if someone is inside, I'll have the element of surprise. The doors open. The lift is empty.

Inside, I glare at the buttons, irritated that I have no idea where to even start the search for Allen and Chandler. The first ten levels are numbered floors, but at the bottom are ones labeled "HYDRO," "OXYGEN," and "OBSERVATORY."

Observatory?

I jam the button. "Bottoms up."

The elevator jerks into motion. As I wait, I flip through the rest of the journal. In the very back is another piece of paper, carefully folded in quarters. At first glance, it looks like a vintage circus flyer with bold lettering announcing entertainment in various fonts and text sizes. My gaze flits back and forth across the page, trying to process it. The elevator lurches, passing levels one…two…

"Allen's Time Voyages: Experience the World's Greatest Disasters!"

"Amazing Adventures!"

"Extraordinary Excursions!"

In the center is a picture of a hovering black sphere: the

Wormhole Device.

My mind races, trying to align what I read in the letter and what this flyer says. Allen's greatest desire was to find Marie. How does a desperate, all-consuming search for one's lost love turn into this?

At the bottom of the page is a heading: "*Our Most Daring Campaigns.*" Beneath it are about a dozen events and dates. I skim through them, barely getting over the shock of one before reading the next. Every single event listed is a Black Date—a date too dangerous, too world-changing for travelers to be present. The *Titanic*—April 15, 1912. The *Hindenburg*—May 6, 1937. Pearl Harbor—December 7, 1941. World Trade Center—September 11, 2001.

The *Continuum*—April 15, 2112.

I'm still staring, stupidly, unable to process what I've just read, when the lift stops and the doors open…directly out into space.

I reel backward, arms pinwheeling, hands grasping for something to keep me from being sucked out of the elevator. Blackness stares up at me from where the floor should be.

Then I notice what I should have seen first: standing less than twenty feet away, hovering above the heavens with an amused look on his face, is Allen himself.

It takes me a moment to realign my senses. Though he appears to be floating triumphantly over a brilliant ocean of stars, it's merely an illusion. The floor beneath him is a solid, glare-free glass.

The glass observatory clings like a soap bubble to the underside of the ship. A few crates are stacked on the far side of the room, long-forgotten and covered in dust. Otherwise, it's empty, probably to provide the most uninterrupted view of space possible.

I understand now why the *Continuum*'s engineers went through so much trouble to make people feel as if they're still on Earth, with the tinted panes that obscure the stars, the Earth-like city, and even the artificial dirt. The truth: space is terrifying. It's beautiful, majestic, and miraculous in its vastness, but from here, standing on the edge where the solid floor meets the glass that opens out into nothingness,

I'm both exhilarated and paralyzed with fear.

As I'm studying the floor, Allen is studying me. I feel the intensity of his gaze and hide the journal and flyer behind my back.

"What have you done with Chandler?" I demand as soon as I find my voice.

"It was you, wasn't it? 1912." It's a statement, not a question. He suddenly looks weary and haggard. His hair is tinged with silver, and the skin around his eyes folds into creases.

"You took Marie." His voice is low and solemn.

"And you took Chandler."

Allen pulls a handkerchief from his suit and dabs his forehead. "That's not quite the same now, is it? When he wakes, I'm sure he'll agree that in this case, he was the one who provoked me, whereas Marie did nothing to harm you in the least."

"She broke the Rules. She didn't belong there."

"You may have a point." His voice cracks. "Indeed, I should be grateful. Did you know that I searched for her? I devoted my life to finding her. Never mind that I was thrust into a future with no knowledge of the place. That I had to learn your silly, crude mannerisms and base slang, not to mention how to operate your infernal computing machines."

That's exactly how I've felt in this future, and I consider telling him that to build a bit of camaraderie. His scathing look makes me rethink that strategy.

"Did you find her?" Unease creeps through me. If Allen hadn't witnessed the Extraction...if he hadn't seen what the Wormhole Device could do... How entangled has the timeline become? And how on earth can I fix it now?

"Oh, yes," he says as he paces. "I found her, and I discovered she was not at all the angelic young beauty I thought she was. You know what she was? How I found her?"

He stops, running a hand through his dark hair in consternation, but I don't respond.

"She was a *floozy*! A depraved woman with no more modesty than a harlot, who sold herself for the entertainment of the masses and a shiny penny in her pocket!" He spits out the accusation, then turns away, as if I, too, am tainted by association.

Of course. The woman he knew as Marie is a rich, bored pop star with a modern, rather provocative image to keep up. Of course her suggestive lyrics and dance moves—not to mention skimpy costumes—would scandalize her Edwardian fiancé. It'd never occurred to me, as I read Allen's letters of admiration and love, that he might find the present-day Marie in a penthouse Jacuzzi, surrounded by her other admirers.

"You spoke with her?"

"I never approached her, after seeing who she really was. I had no desire to seek contact again, not after discovering her deception. Our life together was just a game to her, a diversion bought at a price. After a few months of wallowing in self-pity," he says, screwing his face up in disgust, "I realized that what one woman will pay for, others will as well."

"That's what the flyer is for," I say, finally making the connection. "But why not just go back to 1912? Move on with your life?"

"There was nothing left for me in my own time or in hers."

"So this is what you decided to devote your life to instead?" I ask, holding up the flyer.

As if putting on a mask, the emotion drains from him, leaving only a calm, businesslike stoicism. "Your technology intrigued me but left much to be improved upon. Once the sphere was sufficiently modified, I traveled forward hundreds of years and developed the concept of an enterprise built only on the most daring, sensational stops of all times. With enough hindsight, the itinerary was easy to construct; all that was left was to survey the stops firsthand to make the final preparations for my clients."

With this, he straightens up, smooths out an invisible wrinkle in his impeccable suit, and holds out his hand. "Now, I need your device and my journal. I shall not have you or your companion interfering further."

Reluctantly, I hand over the journal.

"But, disasters? Won't that put your clients in harm's way? And morally, do you really want to profit from someone else's losses?" All this talk reminds me suddenly of the final disaster on the list. "And the *Continuum*—what happens to it?"

To us. Here. Today.

"Did you not profit from *my* loss?"

The words hit me with such a force that I step backwards.

"Marie wasn't being dishonest with you," I say quietly. "Yes, she was a traveler from my time, but she experienced a lapse in her memory. She got caught up in her own story and confabulated a past for herself. It wasn't intentional. In her own mind, she truly believed she belonged there with you in 1912."

"Oh, certainly she did." He leans in toward me, and I fight the urge to retreat. "*After* she visited a hypnotist to alter her memory."

"But, that's…" My voice trails off. The more I consider it, the less impossible it seems. Many people visit hypnotists to 'reprogram' how their minds work regarding fears or addictions. In theory, a hypnotist *could* provide suggestions to make someone believe that their travel in the past was reality and their memories of the future were merely visions or dreams.

"The sphere, please," he says.

I reach into my pockets, my fingers touching not one but two pieces of cold metal. Except Allen only asked for one. I hesitate, thinking through my options. Finally, I pull out one of the Wormhole Devices, relinquishing it with a begrudging scowl and hoping I've made the right choice in keeping the one I have.

"At least tell me where Chandler is," I say.

"He is fine. I don't wish to harm anyone, but I cannot allow either of you to Jump back to my past and prevent me from completing my preparations. You might keep in mind, however, that the *Continuum* is not long for this world—this galaxy, I should say." His smile is cold and unfeeling. "Feel free to keep the flyer as a souvenir."

CHAPTER TWENTY-TWO: APRIL 14, 2112

As if on cue, the floor beneath us shudders, accompanied by an endless grating that seems to come from everywhere at once. The dark underside of a mountainous rock passes far too close to the colony.

An asteroid.

Its mass blocks out the stars on one side of the Observatory, and I feel like an ant watching a boot come down on me. My legs give way and I fall. I curl up, fearful that I won't stop, that I'll keep falling and crash through the glass and into the depths of space. I brace myself for the end. When the quaking finally stops, everything is silent and still.

Allen stands over me. He opens his journal and—turning directly to a page I must have skipped—he reads aloud. "At precisely 22:14 local time, an asteroid strikes the *Continuum*, tearing a mile-long gash in its hull, puncturing the oxygen and water storage tanks, and bringing to pass the greatest disaster of the twenty-second century."

He checks his pocket watch. "Right on time. Excellent." He makes a note in his journal, snaps the book shut, and turns to the glass curvature to watch the asteroid grow smaller, seemingly unmarked by the collision.

"Funny how history repeats itself," he says to himself. I think I see a flicker of something—fear? or sorrow?—in his eyes, but with a blink, it disappears, replaced by steely indifference.

"I realize you are no amateur in these matters," he says, "but if I were you, I would dismiss any thought of interfering with the events transpiring here or with my research of them. In fact, if I so much as see you again in the next two hours, I shall be forced to deal with you harshly. You'd best focus your attention on finding a seat in an escape pod. According to the history books not yet written, at exactly 24:03, the pressure from the fissure becomes too strong, and rends the ship apart. It will be quite a show, but one must get the timing just right."

He touches his finger to his forehead, as if tipping a hat to me, and turns to leave. I grasp for something, *anything* to say, to stop him.

"Funny, I don't think Marie would approve of the person you've become, either."

His jaw clenches and his nostrils flare. Holding out the device, he tosses it into the air like a little boy with a ball, or a juggler warming up for an act. I cringe at the carelessness of the action.

"Is that so?" he asks.

"Please, those are—"

Before I can finish my thought, Allen winds up. With the grace of a dancer and the power of an athlete, he throws the device across the room. As it crashes against the glass surface, I flinch and squeeze my eyes shut.

There's no *whoosh* of air leaving the room, no omnipotent force yanking me off my feet and out to embrace the stars. Slowly, I open my eyes.

While the observatory remains intact, the same can't be said for the Wormhole. The device lies shattered in pieces, metal glittering among the stars. Even the tough outer shell has cracked open, exposing entrails of wires, springs, and Dr. Wells' lifelong work. It lies there, silent and still, its luminous shell now dull and broken, its mysteries exposed and its power stolen.

My hand jerks involuntarily to my pocket, to the reassuring form of the second device. When I look up again, Allen's disappeared into the elevator. On the floor just outside the door is a folded slip of paper I must not have noticed earlier. Did he drop it on his way out?

The paper seems to unfold itself in my hands, without any directives from my brain. My fingers shake as I read the short, concise note.

Chandler—

B+B plan to eliminate you upon your return to the present. They no longer trust you, but you know too much about their operation. My conscience would not allow me to stand idly by. Please take whatever precautions are necessary to prevent this terrible disaster.

Sincerely, a friend.

It's the message Chandler carried around—the reason he didn't want to return to the present. He must have dropped it here, but where is he now?

I reach for the Wormhole in my pocket. My fingertips trace its smooth surface. Now I understand Chandler's earlier hesitation.

I fiddle with my PVD, trying to access the news feeds. There has to be some sort of alert, some instructions for the citizens about what to do in an emergency. When a newscaster finally bursts into view in the corner of my vision, she seems far too calm—no, too bored—for the circumstances.

"—the governing board has verified that the jolt some people felt a few minutes ago was an asteroid brushing the outer surface of the *Continuum*. Though this asteroid was larger than most we've encountered thus far, there is no need for alarm. With its unique outer shell of fortified plastic, this colony is—as the engineers assure us—practically indestructible."

I've heard that before.

CHAPTER TWENTY-THREE: APRIL 14, 2112

Back on the surface, I run. My feet beat out a rhythm, and Rule #7 echoes through my head: "Travelers are prohibited from disclosing any foreknowledge to people of the past."

I don't care. I think of Dodge, back in Apartment Y with his elderly neighbor, sleeping. I could warn him via my PVD, but I don't have time to stop and figure out how, and there are so many other innocent people here, too. I can't let this become another *Titanic*, where people die simply because of what they don't know. I have to alert everyone. And quickly.

Then I can worry about Allen.

The map still floats in my field of vision, and with a few awkward hand gestures, I orient myself. Past the elevator, the agriculture fields dead-end against the colony's outer edge, but over the stalks of corn looms a wall—not the delicate, glass dome of the exterior panels, but a flat, black wall that looks like it's built to endure quite a pounding. According to my map, I've found the Control Center.

I cut through the fields toward the wall. Lines of rivets run up and down its surface, piecing together enormous sheets of an unfamiliar metallic material. At first, I don't see anywhere else to go, but then, a little farther to my left, something catches my eye. It's a door, barely visible, which is made of the same material as the wall. There's no retina scan, no handle, and no knob. Great. An emergency exit, which apparently only opens from the inside.

I kick the door in frustration. I don't have time to waste waiting for someone to come out, and there's no other entrance nearby.

"Think!" I hiss, pacing before the door. I need a better plan, and fast. It's not like the Governing Committee is going to let me waltz in and send the *Continuum*'s citizens into a panic with a doomsday announcement, anyway. In the past, my greatest strength has been my foreknowledge about people and events. Now, even though I know what's going to happen, that insight isn't doing me any good.

Then I spot it: a tiny black dot on the door's upper corner. I stand on tiptoes to get a better look, and a stream of hope surges through me. It's a security camera. I wave my hands before it and shout at the top of my lungs. "Let me in!"

Heavy footfalls on the other side of the door warn me that someone's coming. The door bursts open and I'm suddenly face to face with a man wearing military fatigues and holding a rifle. He blinks in surprise.

Before he can utter a word, I dive between his body and the doorframe. The cold barrel of his gun brushes my elbow as I lunge past him, but that doesn't stop me. My sudden move must've astonished him as much as me, because when he tries to step back, he trips over the threshold and his gun clatters to the floor.

In all my years as a Retriever, I've never acted so recklessly. The adrenaline shooting through me makes me smile like a lunatic as I run. Ahead, a door stands slightly ajar. The guard's in pursuit—stomping and shouting behind me—so I fling myself through the doorway and pull the door shut behind me. The guard is making so much ruckus he probably can't tell that my steps have stopped. He stumbles past and around another corner, breathing heavily.

The room I've shut myself into is a storage closet, full of sharp-smelling cleaning supplies. I pull up the map on my PVD, ducking into a corner so the hologram's glow doesn't spill into the hallway. I find my objective and make note of the turns I'll need to take. Then I swat the map away and look around.

The closet is stuffed full of supplies, and I dig through box after box until I find something I can use as disguise. I pull my hair out of its ponytail, letting it hang down into my face. I throw a rumpled-up vest with a "Continuum Janitorial Services" emblem on it over my suit. A matching cap hides my eyes.

I may not look like an entirely different person, but the guard's the only one who'd recognize me; anyone else might be fooled into thinking I belong here. Sometimes an excessive amount of confidence is the best disguise; pretend you belong, and no one else will doubt you, either.

Raising my chin, I emerge from my hiding place, brandishing a broom and dustpan, and walk briskly. Every hallway in this complex is identical: identical white walls, identical white doors. A tall, dark man with a similar cap walks past me.

"Evening," I say, imitating his sharp nod.

Around the next corner, I find it: the plain, white door marked "FEEDS."

The room is a hive of activity. The outer wall is a giant screen that encircles a dozen workstations. There, technicians observe smaller screens, their hands flying back and forth as they enter information. They look like a dozen feuding maestros conducting a dozen feuding symphonies. Fortunately, they're so engrossed in their work that no one notices me as I pull off the cap and vest and ditch them, along with the broom, beside the door.

The scrolling, scanning, blinking, popping-up, and fading-away messages projected all around are mesmerizing.

"The top ten songs of the day are..."

"...and the stock market dropped another forty points..."

"...won by twenty-nine points after a..."

I scan one workstation and then the next. Finally, I find the technician whose screen displays the information about the asteroid crash. Her eyes flick back and forth along with the acrobatics of her hands, but as she inputs the information about the asteroid—*harmless*, they're still saying—her face remains unaffected.

I close my eyes, contemplating what I'm about to do. I reach out to touch her shoulder, but before it connects, I catch a glimpse of my watch and it gives me pause.

Rule #8.

I don't even belong here. This isn't my era, and the changes I make could still have serious unintended consequences. But I can't sit by and watch; that'd make me no better than Allen.

I touch her shoulder. Bright curls bounce as she turns, her eyebrows scrunched in confusion. "Who are you?"

"The Governing Committee sent me to relay the message in person, so there would be no mistake," I say, my voice firm and commanding. "The asteroid damage is irreparable; we must call for an immediate evacuation."

The room still buzzes with activity. Feeds scroll along on the screen behind the technician, but she remains immobile.

"Did you hear me?" I straighten to my full height and put as much force into my voice as I can. "This evacuation needs to take place *now*. People's lives are at stake."

"But—"

"Do it. Now."

She shrinks beneath my glare and gestures helplessly at the screen. "I...I can't. I'm just a technician. I'm not authorized to put out a red alert."

I bite back a curse. If I'd really been sent by the Governing Committee, I'd have known that. Thinking fast, I lean in, right into her personal space, eking out every ounce of intimidation I possess. "Then find someone who can."

She turns pale but rises from her seat, looking about nervously. I follow her across the room to another work station where a man with salt-and-pepper-hair sits, scowling at his screen.

"Excuse me, Mr. Veltman," she says, her voice uncertain. "I have an officer here reporting an evacuation."

"Evacuation? On whose orders?"

I step back, ready to fade into the shadows if this turns sour as I suspect it might when Redhead's boss realizes I'm obviously not who I say I am.

"Th-the Governing Committee," she stammers, gesturing toward me. "Apparently, that asteroid did more damage than initial reports indicated. The destruction is irreparable."

He looks straight at me. "Is this true?"

"Yes, sir." I force myself to stand upright, not to wilt beneath his piercing gaze. *Please don't ask for my credentials.*

His silence seems endless, then is shattered as he lets loose a curse. "I knew that jolt felt too strong."

His fingers fly, his orchestra of information reaching a crescendo when the words "CODE RED: EVACUATION" and "PROCEED TO THE ESCAPE PODS IN A PROMPT AND ORDERLY MANNER" flash across the wall in bold, red letters.

The effect is immediate. The others stop what they're doing and leap from their stations. All the work that a moment ago was so important is forgotten. The silent symphonies have devolved into a dissonant buzz of panic and confusion.

"I thought they were taking care of the breach—that it was fine."

"It's straight from the Governing Committee." The redhead raises her hands in defense.

This sets off a new round of frantic twitters. I back away slowly, relieved that the message is out. Everyone will be safe in the escape pods before anyone realizes the message didn't really come from the Committee.

The ensuing chaos is perfect for making my escape, but before I can turn, I'm pulled backward and the prick of a needle pierces my neck. My brain, suddenly fuzzy, registers a familiar mustached face looking down upon me before everything goes dark.

CHAPTER TWENTY-FOUR: APRIL 14, 2112

I wake groggily, fighting for mental clarity.

The asteroid. The communication feeds. The injection.

I tug on my hands, but they remain still and slightly numb.

"Elise! Are you awake?"

I jerk about and immediately regret it. My head throbs, and black spots dot my vision. I can't even turn all the way around. "Chandler?"

"No, it's the Pope. Child, I absolve you from your sins."

I groan, both at his joke and at our present situation. We're tied together, back to back on the Observatory floor. At any moment, the breach in the levels above us could split the ship wide open, and we'd be sucked out into space.

"Chandler, we don't have time for small talk. Allen—"

"Yeah, I know," Chandler says. "I was here earlier, behind those crates with a handkerchief shoved in my mouth and a splitting headache."

"So you heard everything?"

"I was on the verge of blacking out, but I got the gist. You'd think with all the technology here Allen would come up with something better than tying us up with rope."

"We surprised him. He was ready for me later, though, with that injection."

"Did you warn everyone?" His voice wavers.

"Yeah." My gut lurches again. However this turns out, I'm partially responsible.

"Dodge should have his PVD on; he sleeps with it when I'm out at night, in case I need to get a hold of him." Chandler shifts, and the rope digs into my skin, burning the tender area around my wrists.

"Hey, that hurts!"

"Sorry. I guess I should have paid more attention to those old James Bond movies."

"What?" How can he joke around, even now?

"Look, I know you spend a lot of time attending balls and riding in chariots and whatnot, but how do you not know who James Bond is?"

"I know who he is," I say, though admittedly, the part about the balls and chariots is true. "I just don't see how it's relevant."

"He always found some crazy way to escape from these kinds of situations. Hey! We could burn the rope like Indiana Jones."

"Do you have anything to start a fire?"

"Nope. You?"

"Nope." I scan the room. There has to be something. "Wait…I think I've got it."

"What?"

"Allen smashed a Wormhole Device in here. The broken outer shell will have sharp edges. Can you get to the pieces?"

The ropes tighten again as Chandler strains to look across the floor. "Wait, I see them. You'll have to help me scoot over there." He shifts to reposition himself. "On the count of three. One, two, three."

We inch toward the elevator, pressing against each other's backs and walking out our legs in an awkward crab-crawl. It takes longer than expected and much longer than Indiana Jones would've taken, but eventually we make it, panting with exertion.

"I can almost reach it." His back presses into mine as he extends his leg. It takes a few tries, but then he exclaims, "Got it!"

The shard grinds along the glass floor. Chandler struggles against the bonds, and I shift with him, trying to avoid being crushed.

He fumbles around, trying to get a good grip on it. He curses, and it rattles back onto the floor. Warm blood trickles down my hand, and I jerk in surprise.

"Hold still." He grits his teeth and reaches for it again.

"Maybe this wasn't such a good idea…" I say, but when no other options come to mind, I fall silent.

"This isn't as easy as it looks in the movies," Chandler says, still working away at the bindings. I bite my lip, trying to hold still despite the slickness tracing the lines of my hands. Any movement might cause the makeshift blade to sink into my own skin, which makes me woozy just thinking about it.

"How long was I out?" I ask. "We only have until just after midnight."

"Not long; maybe five minutes or so." The moments tick by, agonizingly slow. Finally, the ropes snap into two pieces, and we break apart like polarized magnets. "All right, Cinderella, let's get out of here."

I rub my wrists. They're red and sore, but fortunately, the bindings didn't break the skin. "Cinderella? That's the best you could come up with?"

He smiles through a grimace. Blood drips from his left hand. "It was the midnight reference. I had to go with it. Don't tell me you don't know that story."

"The Cinderella story has been around for centuries. I've probably heard more versions of it than you have. Here, let me see."

I pry Chandler's fist open to get a good look at his cut. The jagged edges open to reveal muscle underneath. The raw, red sight makes me ill.

"We need to clean this out."

"No time." He points to my watch, which says 22:53. We have a little over an hour. Chandler touches his face.

"No, no, no," he says, looking around in panic.

"What? What happened? Stop flinging that arm around; you're going to pull the cut open even more."

"He took our PVDs."

"Don't you think we have bigger things to worry about right now?" I sit on the floor, pull off one of my boots, and peel away my sock. Synthetic materials must've come a long way in the last hundred years, because it's still dry and smells clean, despite the sweat shimmering on my skin.

"Without the PVD, I can't contact Dodge." Desperation fills Chandler's eyes with frightening intensity. "You have to help me find him. I promise, once he's safely on one of those escape pods, you can do whatever you need to with me."

I wind the sock around Chandler's palm as tightly as I can, avoiding eye contact. His offer is clear: his life for Dodge's.

"Keep pressure on that." I tug my boot back on. "Let's run."

The lift lurches beneath us, and Chandler and I exchange a look. All lightheartedness dissolves as the peril of the situation hits us. This elevator shaft is near the damaged portion of the ship, the section that will only hold for another hour before it tears the colony to shreds. Assuming that our presence won't somehow hasten the destruction.

I don't exhale until the doors creak open.

As soon as we step onto solid ground, something snaps behind us. Before the doors even shut, the lift drops out of sight. A crash echoes under our feet and throws us to the ground. Plumes of dust burst from the diminishing crack as the doors slide shut again. The harsh smoke, reeking of chemicals, burns my eyes and throat.

Chandler pulls me up and together we dash toward the escape pods. The Wormhole bounces against my thigh, and I'm tempted to press my thumb against the button, to yank myself back to my own time, except…

I stumble as I realize what I've done to myself. When Allen asked for the device, I gave him *mine*, thinking I could send Chandler back to TUB and Dr. Wells could simply send another Retriever for me later. But there will be no 'later' for the *Continuum*, and without my Wormhole, I need one of those escape pod seats as much as anyone else.

"You okay?" Chandler asks, seeing that I've fallen behind.

"Yeah, go on ahead. I'll catch up. I'm just a little out of shape." Another lie.

He shoots me a frown of concern but takes off, even faster than before. I pull out the device and punch my thumb against the button, knowing it's pointless. The security lock prevents anyone except Chandler from using it, including me.

My feet feel like lead, but I pick them up and race toward the escape pods.

The crowd is visible from a distance. My limbs are already numb and achy, but I grit my teeth and push on to catch up with Chandler. He's a few yards ahead, clutching his bandaged hand to his chest and shouting Dodge's name.

An enormous panel of the hangar bay has been retracted, and the crowd funnels in, arranging themselves according to their apartment's letter designation. Officials bearing firearms scan each person's retina before allowing them into the pod.

I hang back, focused on the lines nearest to me. These final ones—X and Y—are the shortest by far. Are the colony's most elderly members still asleep in their beds? Or struggling to make the trek from the solar train?

A few older men gather off to one side, talking in low voices and shaking their heads. It brings to mind depictions of the *Titanic*'s last moments, of the gentlemen who remained onboard after kissing their loved ones goodbye.

"I've seen mosh pits more organized than this," Chandler says. He scans the crowd, and I join him, shouting Dodge's name over the din.

"He should be here, by the pod for apartment Y."

"Maybe they put him in another line because he's a minor."

"Maybe." He looks doubtful.

"I'll check the other lines."

I push through the crowd. Someone bumps into me, nearly knocking me over in a mad desperation to fight his way to the front of the line. An infant peers over his mother's shoulder, his eyes wide. She gently pushes his head into her chest, trying to shield him from the chaos. The noise drowns out any intelligible conversation. Individual words muddle together, churning in a sea of panic and confusion.

Suddenly, one face stands out, as if illuminated by a spotlight. He wears the same suit as everyone else, yet it hangs on his frame with an unexpected elegance. Though the crowd pushes and shoves, he stands like a boulder in a stream, silent and still. He watches those around him, and his hardened features fracture. One moment, he's frozen; the next is as if he's awoken, recognizing where he is and what's happening around him. He looks up and meets my eyes. In that moment, amid all the commotion, we are still, silent, and connected.

We're two travelers, standing at opposite ends of the maddening crowd, drawn together by our common past, our shared present, and our knowledge of the future, yet separated by all that's happened between us. The moment passes, pushed out of existence by the moment that succeeds it. Allen lifts his hand—a tip of a hat from another time—then turns and disappears into the crowd.

Someone grabs me. It's Chandler, beside me again. "Elise, I just realized… You're not in the system. You don't have an apartment assignment. You're not supposed to be here, and the diplomat ships? You'd better believe those were the first to leave."

Technically speaking, he's not supposed to be here either, but then it dawns on me what he's saying. He's added himself to the system, but I'm not on any *Continuum* manifests—as a citizen or a diplomat. I don't have a seat on the pods; there won't be room for me. I *have* to

Extract. I glance back to where Allen disappeared into the crowd.

I have one last chance.

"Go," I say. "Find Dodge. Get to an escape pod. I'll find you again if I can."

"But—" He reaches for me, looking pointedly at the suit's pocket where I carry the Wormhole.

Ignoring him, I take off, threading my way through the crowd, desperately searching for the one person I'd never wanted to see again.

CHAPTER TWENTY-FIVE: APRIL 14, 2112

When I burst out of the launch bay, the stagnant, sweat-filled air clears and—to my alarm—it feels thinner. Something's not right with the colony's atmosphere. I work harder at each breath than I'm used to. The difference is subtle, and most people wouldn't notice it, especially in their current panic.

Too many minutes have passed. It's almost time for whatever strength of engineering is holding this colony together to crumble, and anyone not in one of the escape pods—or in another time—will be sucked out into space.

I scan the buildings, searching for any hint of movement. Finally, I see him. He stands near a small warehouse away from the crowd, but still within sight. His head is hunched over, staring at a piece of paper in his hand. As I watch, he pulls a cigarette lighter from his pocket and ignites the paper's edge. The smoldering sheet flutters down, slowly disintegrating into smoke and ash.

I approach as I would an injured animal. When he takes out another object, a gasp escapes my lips. He's either deep in thought or the crowd is still too loud even at this distance, because he doesn't notice. I quicken my pace, afraid of what he might do next.

He raises an upturned palm with the orb balanced gently atop it.

In the dimly-lit nighttime panels, Allen's Wormhole looks liquid and strangely alive. His hand wavers.

"Don't!" My voice catches in my throat, the intensity of the cry tearing at my vocal cords, as if the blunt force of my word could still his hand.

I lunge to close the distance between us. My hands shoot out to break the device's fall, but I'm still meters away when the delicate lifeline shatters on the *Continuum*'s uncompromising surface.

The crash echoes in my ears. Tiny fragments dance across the ground. Springs pirouette and wires leap as I fall to my knees, still too far away to reach the scattering shards. They land among the paper's ashes; all that remains is one small corner. *"Our Most Daring Campaigns."*

When the last glitters have stilled and the tinkling of broken dreams reaches a full stop, I find my voice. "Why?"

Allen looks up, stupefied, as if seeing me for the first time. "You should be on a pod."

"Why did you destroy it?"

"My ambition," he whispers. "I thought it would be an adventure, but I realize now what a monster I've become."

He turns away, a hand over his mouth as if the very thought has made him physically ill. "What sort of fiend would want to witness that suffering? I had to be stopped." He turns to me, his skin now so pale that it makes him seem untouchable, like a china doll on a shelf. "I lied."

"What?"

"The letter I wrote to Marie." He hangs his head. "I know you read it. Most of it was true, but I couldn't face my cowardice. I'd only imagined that I'd had the courage to stand and look death in the eye as the ship sunk into the sea.

"I was terrified. I panicked. I jumped over the edge. I thought I could land in one of the lifeboats as it was lowered, but I misjudged the distance and hit the water instead." He shudders. "I clutched the one object of any value to me: Marie's sphere. I'd already disabled the locking mechanism, and when I went under, I must have pressed the button. The next thing I knew, it pulled me through time."

He starts choking up, and I rise to my feet, uncertain whether I should comfort him or keep my distance.

"If you were so terrified, why come here, of all places?" I ask. Anyone could see the similarities between the two events. History was repeating itself.

"I read about the men's bravery. Even my own brother, who'd never done a single noble thing in his life... Even he wasn't as selfish and cowardly as I was." Allen squeezes his eyes shut. "History describes him helping women and children into the lifeboats. When they had all launched, he pulled up a deck chair and lit his pipe, accepting his fate."

Allen crumples to his knees, pulling at his hair. I remain silent.

"I had to do it," he whispers. "I had to come here...to see for myself...to prove I'm not a coward. But I am. A coward of the worst sort."

His weary body folds in on itself. This man whom I've thought of as twisted and cruel is really just broken. My emotions are confused, but bitterness still grumbles within me, refusing him any expression of compassion. By condemning himself to go down with this ship, he sealed my fate as well.

I turn to walk away, but he pleads, "Forgive me."

CHAPTER TWENTY-SIX: APRIL 15, 2112

A sudden change in the crowd's pitch distracts me. Back at the launch bay, there are only two escape pods remaining.

Chandler. Dodge.

Without a glance back at Allen, I run toward the pods.

We have mere minutes before the end of the *Continuum*, and there are still thirty or forty people who haven't boarded an escape pod. What's going on?

The air is eerily quiet and thin. My eyes burn with the residual fumes of the pods' rocket fuel. I push through the diminished crowd, past those who have come to grips with not leaving. Though there's still the odd person here or there whose countenance is filled with panic or anger, the majority of those remaining—mostly officers and other men—have the same sorrowful look of resignation.

Even with my warning, I wasn't able to save everyone. I glance around at the crowd, trying to rectify what went wrong. Were there not enough seats? Or were there pods that—just like the *Titanic*'s lifeboats—left prematurely, without their full capacity? As I look into each face, I wonder if I've actually changed the outcome at all.

The final pod is being loaded in the last tube. Tube Y. The officials have drawn their guns and are holding back a few people still fighting to reach it. When I press forward, a hand settles on my shoulder—a gray-haired stranger who shakes his head to discourage my fight toward the officials.

"I just need to say goodbye." Finally, I reach the front of the crowd. Over the officials' heads, I find the faces I've been searching for. "Chandler!"

Dodge spots me, returning my greeting with an enthusiastic wave. Fortunately, he's still too young to fully grasp the situation's magnitude. Chandler strides over, parting the guards so we're face to face.

"Dodge is safe," he says.

"Thank God—"

"I'm ready to go back."

"But—"

"I've said my goodbyes. We don't have a lot of time, so give me the Wormhole and I'll Extract from here."

"But—"

"It's okay. It's not like anyone here is going to talk." His eyes shift to the handful of people around us, and the pity in them mirrors my own emotions.

"Enough," the official in front of us says, needlessly loud. "Back to the pod, or we'll give your seat to someone else."

Chandler opens his mouth to respond, but I interrupt.

"You can't Extract. Your devices were both smashed. The first one when you were fighting Allen, and the other broke in the Observatory. I only have mine left." I pull it out, brandishing it as proof that only one remains. Fortunately, he has no way to know whose it is.

"What about Rule #1?" The corner of his mouth turns up slightly. "If I board one of those escape pods, there's no going back. We both know I don't belong here."

I look over his shoulder at the dark-haired face peering out from the escape pod. "I think this is exactly where you belong. Take care of him, okay?"

"Final call!"

Chandler wraps his arms around me, and I let him embrace me, willing my heartbeat to slow down, so as not to expose my lies. He lets go and hurries back to the pod, where he buckles himself next to Dodge. Chandler whispers to him, and whatever he says must reassure the boy. Dodge grins at me, waving as if he's on an amusement park ride.

With tears threatening to fall, I back slowly away.

The door closes on the final escape pod. The tube's airlock hisses shut. I can't pull my gaze from the last window of the pod and the blue eyes that look back at me with confidence, even a hint of excitement, as Chandler bursts out of his past and into the future that awaits him. The image sears itself into my mind.

I'll never forget it.

"Good luck," I whisper. In moments, the pod's momentum will push it out of sight until the *Continuum* is barely a speck in the myriad of stars that will swallow it up. I wonder if Chandler will look back at the implosion.

A hand touches my forearm and I tense, surprised to see Allen's face so near mine. I pull away, my hand automatically moving to protect the hip pocket where the Wormhole—useless to anyone without Chandler's thumbprint—rests.

Allen puts up his hands. "Please, wait."

I look him in the eyes, eyes that now only show sorrow and loss, and perhaps a twinge of fear. "What do you want?"

"You lied to him."

"I lie to a lot of people." I eye him suspiciously. "How did you know?"

"If you could use the device, would you still be here talking to me? May I see it?"

I hold the Wormhole flat in my palm. Allen takes it carefully, studying it for a moment before looking up.

"I can fix this."

"What? How?"

"Removing the security mechanism was the first thing I did with Marie's. It's a simple matter of snipping the correct wires."

"Do we have enough time?" I barely dare to hope.

Allen looks around. A large metal crate sits off to one side of the launch bay, and he hurries over to it. He takes a small toolkit from his suit pocket and unties the piece of ocean-blue ribbon holding the leather pouch together.

"Is there anything I can do to help?" I ask.

Allen places his pocket watch next to the device. "Watch the time. We have ten minutes."

I beg the second hand to slow down. The floor pitches, and the Wormhole slips out of Allen's grasp, rolling toward the edge of the box. He curses and snatches it up before it can fall, then pries on it with a tiny scalpel-like tool.

Four minutes pass, then five, six. I've gnawed my fingernails into nubs by the time Allen makes the final *snip* with his wire-cutters and snaps the device's outer shell into place. He holds it out, a peace offering and my only hope for survival. Though I know TUB will be waiting for me, as I take hold of the device, I feel strangely optimistic.

Allen snaps his pocket watch shut and holds it out to me. An intricate etching of a ship embellishes the front. It's incredibly old and probably expensive. Before I can ask, he speaks. "I don't deserve any kindness from you, but please, could you get this to Marie?"

I hesitate, not wanting to make promises I can't keep. "I'll try."

Over my shoulder, something catches his eye, and I turn around. Near the empty launch tubes, the men who'd gathered earlier have formed a tired semi-circle and seem to be discussing something important. One man—the shortest and most wrinkled—clears his throat and hums a single tone. With the angelic harmony of a choir, the small enclave begins to sing.

Nearer, my God, to Thee, nearer to Thee!
E'en though it be a cross that raiseth me;
Still all my song would be nearer, my God, to Thee!

Allen straightens up, his back braced against the impact to come. His expression is calm, but his eyes are glazed. He catches me watching him.

"Go." His tone is encouraging, confident, as if in this moment he's instilling in me all the hopes and dreams of happiness that he had harbored for himself. Just as I had watched Chandler go, desiring only the best for him and his new life, Allen now offers me the same blessing.

Though like the wanderer, the sun gone down,
Darkness be over me, my rest a stone;
Yet in my dreams I'd be nearer, my God, to Thee,
Nearer, my God, to Thee, nearer to Thee!

"Marie wanted you to know..." I struggle to recall her exact words. "That she'll always treasure the days with you at the seaside. She wanted you to be happy." It isn't an eloquent eulogy, but it's what he needs to hear.

His eyes close and a single tear slides down his cheek. It shatters his calm countenance; his face contorts in sorrow. "Thank you."

There let the way appear steps unto heav'n
All that Thou sendest me in mercy giv'n;

I hold out the Wormhole. "I wish..."

Allen raises a hand. He shakes his head. He's faced death before, but this time he's prepared.

Angels to beckon me nearer, my God, to Thee,

Nearer, my God, to Thee, nearer to Thee!

My thumb finds the ridge of the device's button. I study it, trying to read it like a crystal ball. What future waits for me back in 2012?

Or if on joyful wing, cleaving the sky,
Sun, moon, and stars forgot, upwards I fly,

Allen steps back, the same awe and wonderment filling his eyes as the first time he watched me disappear in 1912. This time he won't follow. It was his own choices that led him here. Acceptance sits nobly upon his brow as he joins in the final lines:

Still all my song shall be, nearer, my God, to Thee,
Nearer, my God, to Thee, nearer to Thee!

I press the button and feel the familiar tingle of the earth giving way beneath me, the nauseating pressure that reminds me I'm not really where I belong, that another time is calling me home. Tears flood my eyes.

My gaze meets his. He smiles gently. The tug at my heart is only outweighed by the omnipotent tug of time, pulling me away from the eruption of light and sound that rips through my senses. Is it the fabric of time or the final death cry of the *Continuum*? All I know is that I'll never forget it.

THE PRESENT

CHAPTER TWENTY-SEVEN: APRIL 15, 2012

The shining world of the future spins away. Those dark eyes, filled with weary acceptance are burned into my eyelids. In another time, under different circumstances, could he have been happy? Was it our interference that led him to that end? The uncertainty gnaws at me.

Suddenly, there's gray carpet beneath my head. I must've been more distracted than I thought; I never lose my footing on Extractions anymore. Piles of notebooks and papers surround me. Familiar, and definitely *not* the TUB headquarters.

A pair of loafers leaps out from behind the desk. Dr. Wells' face is creased with worry, but I couldn't be more relieved to see him.

"Elise! Thank goodness!" He helps me up, studying my features for clues. "Something went wrong."

I flop onto the edge of a chair, even now mindful not to disturb his piles. I don't know how to feel. I've failed TUB. I've failed PITTA. I've failed Dr. Wells, and I've broken the Rules I held sacred. Despite all of that, I don't regret what I've done.

"I failed."

Over the next half hour, I recount the events of my trip. I tell him what happened to me and Chandler over the past days and how it's changed everything.

"And then you Extracted back here," Dr. Wells says when I've finished.

"But how? The Wormhole was supposed to take me to TUB's headquarters."

"I had to ensure that you found your way here before TUB got a hold of you, so I reprogrammed your Wormholes. I wasn't sure it would work or that I'd have the time to complete the reprogramming, so I left you the warning message in case."

Should I be offended that my boss and mentor, who relied on me for so many cases in the past, didn't think I'd be able to complete this task? Then again, he programmed *both* devices back here. He'd known more than I'd thought.

I reach into my pocket and pull out Chandler's letter, pressing it open onto the table. "You warned him."

"I had no idea how this would turn out. I slipped it in his pocket before he Jumped the second time. I didn't know they'd send a Retriever after him."

"I don't suppose... Couldn't we still make things right somehow, for everyone? Allen, too? I mean, we *do* have a time machine."

Dr. Wells turns to me, the pain on his face fresh and raw. "Don't you see? It's already done."

"So it's unchangeable? What about free will? Personal choice? Is everything really *fated* to happen?" Bitter tears sting my eyes as I recall Allen's last moments.

"No, no." He holds up a hand. "The decisions we make dictate the life we lead. We each made our choices here: me, Agent Chandler, and you. And from what you've told me, I'm proud of the ones you made."

But now what? I have to get away before TUB discovers me, but I have nowhere to go. I can't hide from them forever. "If only I could disappear into the past."

"Let's think this through." The creases on his face deepen. "I'll convince TUB to Jump the next Retriever to somewhere on Earth's surface, instead of Jumping to the *Continuum* itself. He will report what happened to the colony, and that will settle it. They'll assume you and Agent Chandler perished in the disaster. We can provide you a new identity..."

"And if they suspect we escaped? They're not just going to give up, are they?"

Dr. Wells sighs. "No, I'm afraid you're right. They eliminated Mike because of what he knew of their secret project; from what you've told me, you know even more than he did."

"And this will be the first place they'll look for me. I have to leave."

"Come then," he says resignedly. "One more choice."

In the Jump preparation room, Dr. Wells opens the door of my wardrobe. I touch the wool, silk, cotton, and linen items, each one calling to mind a particular place and time. I weigh the pros and cons of each.

"Here."

When I see what Dr. Wells is holding, my stomach drops. I take the navy blue traveling gown from him, carefully checking the skirts for any residual dampness from my recent dip in the Southampton harbor.

"Don't you think I ought to go further back? Won't it be safer?"

"You know the Gilded Age better than you do the present, and I doubt TUB would be able to pick you out from among all the other new immigrants. It will work. I know." When I look into his eyes, I see a certainty there I wasn't expecting. "I always knew I'd have to give you up at some point. I just didn't think it'd be so soon."

It takes me a moment to digest what he's telling me, but when it dawns on me, I feel lightheaded.

"You know something about me. About my future...in the past."

"I do."

The words hit me like a slap in the face, and I forget to breathe. Black spots dance across my line of vision, reminding me of my need for oxygen.

"Why didn't you tell me?"

"It wasn't relevant before. Besides, you wouldn't have believed me."

"What about the Rules? The time-space continuum? Don't you care how this could affect the timeline?"

"It's already been done. I wouldn't allow it if I weren't positive. The Rules have to be broken. You have to break them."

I try to read his eyes—big and bright and eager, as if he really wants to, *needs* to tell me what he's kept a secret for so long.

"Tell me what you know."

He sits, but his hands remain in motion, tapping on his thighs and furling and unfurling.

"My grandmother was the only child of two German immigrants. She used to tell me wonderful stories about her childhood in New York. She loved it there, but when her parents died in an apartment fire, she needed a fresh start, so she headed west.

"She arrived one day in the same small town where my grandfather's family lived. When my grandfather returned home from school out east, they met at church and, well..." He smiles, a faraway look in his eyes. "They always said it was love at first sight. They were the kind of couple that people call soul mates."

Despite my aversion to romantic sentimentality, Dr. Wells' story strikes a nerve.

"What does this have to do with me?" The words nearly choke me; it's obvious, but I need to hear it aloud.

When he looks at me, I can see the admiring little boy he once was, glowing in innocent joy at his grandparents' love. He clears his throat and continues.

"My wife, rest her soul, loved genealogy. When she researched my lineage, the facts didn't add up. There was no evidence of my grandmother's existence prior to 1900—no birth certificate, no baptism records. There were no records of her parents, either, nor the fire that took their lives. No census records, ship manifests, newspapers, or immigration documents. It was like one day, she simply…appeared."

"And you're trying to tell me that your grandmother…?" I can't even finish the thought.

"I've carried her picture with me since the day I met you."

He pulls out his wallet. Behind an aged photograph of his wife is another picture. The fragile black and gray portrait, though faded with time, shows a young woman only slightly older than I am now. She wears a dark gown with full sleeves and a high collar, and her hair is pulled back. A secret, Mona Lisa-smile plays around her lips. The plain, round face is too familiar to deny. It's the same face I see every time I look into the mirror, the same hint of a smile I betray every time I'm told *not* to smile.

"When I met you at the convention," Dr. Wells says, "I thought the similarity was a coincidence. The more I got to know you, the more undeniable it was. I wasn't going to tell you, but I don't know how else to assure you that it will all be okay, that this is the right decision."

"And if I change my mind? Decide to go somewhere else instead?"

"You won't. Don't you understand?"

I understand all too well.

I don't *want* to know how it all ends. I can't bear the thought of spending my next years just waiting for it all to transpire, waiting to reach the final pages of the book already spoiled for me. I don't want to know my own future, even if it will be a happy one.

But what's done can't be undone, and I can't forget all I know…

Then it occurs to me. Maybe I *don't* have to spend the rest of my life going through the motions like I'm reading a script. Maybe there's another way.

"I'll go. But there's something I need to do first."

CHAPTER TWENTY-EIGHT: APRIL 15, 2012

The danger of TUB discovering I'm back in 2012 weighs on my mind. I hurry, constantly searching for dark-suited, sunglass-shaded agents. Finally, I arrive at the hotel—one of those ritzy ones owned by some famous millionaire.

The receptionist calls the penthouse, frowning as if it's against her better judgment to relay my message. I glance over my shoulder at the windows that open onto the street. The pinpricks of color from the street lights and taxis shimmer like stars. In the darkness, it's like looking out into space. My mind wanders again to Chandler.

The receptionist hangs up. "Top level."

When I arrive on the top floor, the elevator doors slide open. I hesitate, feeling out of place here.

Marie steps out from another room—tall, elegant, and incredibly modern. In her tailored suit with its plunging neckline and her bright red sandals with three-inch heels, she looks just like the image on her CD covers.

"Have a seat," she says, showing a hint of her previous façade's poise. As she sits across from me, I notice the slight tremble of her hand, the way she avoids eye contact.

"I'm here unofficially," I say. "I don't work for PITTA anymore."

She raises her perfectly-sculpted eyebrows. "Oh?"

"I delivered your message." I'm uncertain whether I should apologize for the pain I caused her back in 1912 or attempt to justify it. It strikes me how much we're alike, caught between eras.

She turns away, trying to hide her tears.

"He wanted you to have this." I hand her the pocket watch, uncertain how to continue. What good would it do to tell the truth of what he discovered when he found her, how it had smashed the pedestal he'd placed her on, and how that disappointment had changed him?

"He loved you very much. Right up until the end."

She smiles ruefully, the pain in her eyes shining through the spite. "He's gone, is he?"

I nod. Again, I'm the bearer of bad news, and the pain is still as raw as the last time I shared information that would break her heart. I want to slip out, to leave her to her grief, but I need her help.

"How much do you remember of what happened in 1912?" I ask.

"All of it, now. It's insane, looking back, that I forgot about...about *now*." She snaps the pocket watch shut.

"Would you mind telling me more about the hypnosis? Please?"

She narrows her eyes, as if suspecting a trap, but she must sense my desperation, because ever so slowly, she nods.

"I should really thank my life coach for the idea," she says. "Before my trip, I was trying to clean up my life, and she suggested hypnosis to help me quit smoking. I went to a hypno-therapist, learned some self-hypnosis. Six weeks later, I'd broken the habit."

She smiles wryly, pulling out a pack of Virginia Slims and lighting one up. "Well, I *did*, anyway, until I went back in time and forgot those sessions." She coughs and extinguishes the cigarette with a sigh. "I get mixed signals now."

"So," I say, "You saw a hypnotist after you Jumped and then sailed overseas, convinced that you were an American heiress."

"When the man at your agency warned me about the possibility of memory troubles and that whatever-you-call-it—"

"Confabulation?"

"That's it. Confabulation. When I heard about it, I immediately thought of how my hypno-therapist altered my mindset and wondered if I could apply the one to achieve the other. I worried that I wouldn't be able to find anyone to help me. When I walked into the hypnotist's office in 1912, though, he acted like it was no big deal. We met daily, and I practiced self-hypnosis on the voyage to Europe. By the time I emerged from my cabin, I wasn't pretending to be someone else, I *was* someone else. Or so I thought."

"Can you give me his name? The hypnotist you saw in 1912?"

She hesitates, then scribbles a name and address onto a takeout menu. As she hands it to me, she tilts her head, squinting slightly as if picturing me in an entirely new light.

"At the time, I wondered why Dr. Mooney believed me so easily," she says, not breaking eye contact. "When I asked, he gave the strangest response. He told me that ten years before, another young lady had requested the same thing."

CHAPTER TWENTY-NINE: APRIL 15, 2012

"You took care of what you needed to do?" Dr. Wells asks as he enters the Jump prep room.

"Yes, thank you."

Dr. Wells' eyes linger on mine, and I know he wants to ask me where I was, but this secret is best kept between Marie and me. I fumble at the drawstring of my handbag.

"I hope this will suffice; it was all I had available for that era." He hands me a thin stack of paper bills.

"I'm grateful for anything you could spare—" I stop as I catch the amount of each: $500.

"I can't." I push the money back into his hands. "Each of these is worth a year's wages in the early 1900s."

"I need to know you'll be okay." He closes my fingers around the notes. I hesitate, then tuck them into my handbag. At least I won't be destitute.

"I'll be okay," I assure him. I clutch the takeout menu in my pocket—the one with the address that will help me forget all this—and take a deep breath.

"The Box is ready." Dr. Wells clears his throat. "Whenever you are."

The year is set to 1902. My entire future is built around the conviction that somehow, I'll find my way to the unknown little town where I'll meet the young scholar who will sweep me off my feet. He certainly has his work cut out for him. I don't know where that will be, or when, but the butterflies fluttering in my stomach make me realize, for the first time, that I'm looking forward to it.

"I'm ready." And I am ready. Ready for my life to begin. I step into the Box.

I'm going home.

The unchecked thought surprises me. A home. A lifelong love. A family of my own.

My handbag is strangely light without the Wormholes' weight; my feet could float right off the ground. Dr. Wells stands outside the door. At the last moment, he hesitates and pulls me in for a hug. It's awkward, knowing who he is now. How strange these past years must've been for him.

"Were you close to... Were we close?" I ask, hoping he understands what I mean.

"My grandmother was extraordinary. She used to tell me stories about climbing into a box and visiting the future. She said it was a dream she'd have sometimes. That's where I got the idea for the DeLorean Box." He pauses, choking up. "I'll miss you."

With his simple explanation, my vision blurs. Standing before me, in the body of an elderly man, is a little boy who's losing his beloved grandmother all over again. I'm frozen in place, immobilized by the realization that this final Jump will set so much in motion.

I lean forward and kiss him on the forehead. "Thank you. For everything."

Releasing his hand, I step into the Box.

Dr. Wells flips the switch and steps back. With one hand, I grip the handrail. The other rests on the glass: a silent, final goodbye.

ABOUT THE AUTHOR

Wendy Nikel is a speculative fiction author with a degree in elementary education, a fondness for road trips, and a terrible habit of forgetting where she's left her cup of tea. Her short fiction has been published by *Fantastic Stories of the Imagination*, *Daily Science Fiction*, *Nature: Futures*, and various other anthologies and e-zines. For more info, visit wendynikel.com or subscribe to her newsletter!

Watch for A Place in Time, Book #2: *The Grandmother Paradox*, available fall 2018! And turn the page for some questions to jumpstart your discussion of *The Continuum*.

DISCUSSION QUESTIONS

1. Elise considers the Rules of utmost importance and shows irritation at clients who don't share her convictions. Are there any "rules" in your life (societal, social, moral, religious) that you strictly adhere to? What's your view of people who don't follow these same rules?

2. Allen's brother wanted him recognize Marie's lies on his own, rather than cause contention by pointing out her story's inconsistencies. Do you think this was a wise plan to preserve their brotherly relationship or should he have told Allen what he knew?

3. *Confabulation* is "the replacement of a gap in a person's memory by a falsification that he believes to be true." Even among healthy people, false memories, caused by the process in which the brain encodes information, can commonly occur. Have you ever experienced a memory (perhaps about your childhood) which later you discovered was not true or wasn't quite as you remembered it?

4. A travel agency in the Jack Finney short story "Of Missing Persons" was the inspiration for PITTA. Both agencies are shrouded in secrecy and certain rules that must be followed. Would you travel through time, knowing that you'd be sworn to secrecy and wouldn't be able to share the experience with anyone else?

5. Despite his strict rules, Dr. Wells collects gifts from clients which the world considers "lost" in history. Do you believe that keeping these items is justifiable?

6. Dr. Wells had told Elise that travel to the future was impossible. What might his reasons have been for this falsehood? Which would you believe to be more dangerous: time travel to the future or to the past?

7. When Allen arrives on the *Titanic*'s 100th anniversary commemorative cruise, he finds the event distasteful. Are there any ways that people currently commemorate history that you find distasteful or disrespectful? How do you think the more somber parts of history ought to be remembered?

8. Elise has been so engrossed in the past that when she arrives in the future, one of the things that proves problematic is the use of technology. How has technology and the way we use it changed during your lifetime? Which of these technological advances was the most difficult for you to master?

9. Elise and Chandler discuss some theories of time travel and ponder the role of fate and free will. Which do you consider more likely: A changeable timeline where travelers can alter their present (like in *Back to the Future*)? Or a static one, in which what's happened in the past is fated to happen (like in *The Time Traveler's Wife*)?

10. Elise finds that the people of the future are housed according to age and stage of life. What advantages would there be to a housing system like this? What disadvantages?

11. One of the themes of this story is finding a place where you belong. What gives a person a sense of belonging in a particular place (or time)? If you've moved to a new home, what things have helped you feel like you belong there?

12. Do you believe that Elise will find peace at the end? Why or why not?

ACKNOWLEDGEMENTS

This story has been through a lot to get here, and I'm incredibly grateful to everyone who helped me along the way.

Thanks to my family for their support—my husband and my boys who've been here for me through the ups and downs; my parents who first encouraged my love of reading and writing; and my siblings and extended family who've shared my excitement.

Thanks to my critique partners extraordinaire, who've stuck and pushed me with each draft to become a better writer—S. L. Saboviec, Diane McIntire Rose, Nicole Mogavero, and Rebecca M. Latimer.

Thanks to everyone else who's read and critiqued any of the various forms this story has taken and have helped it become what it is today—Eva Greenleigh, Laurie Gienapp, Brandon Steenbock, Richard Norris, Amy Dionne, Sarah Henning, Aaron T. Smith, and others. Special thanks also to the COSROCK book club for help with the discussion questions and for the Kent District Library for running the short story contest that started this all.

And finally, thanks to those at World Weaver Press for taking a chance on this story—my editor Rhonda Parrish; publisher Sarena Ulibarri; and publicist Kristen Bates.

Thank you for reading!

We hope you'll leave an honest review at Amazon, Goodreads, or wherever you discuss books online.

Leaving a review means a lot for the author and editors who worked so hard to create this book.

Please sign up for our newsletter for news about upcoming titles, submission opportunities, special discounts, & more.

WorldWeaverPress.com/newsletter-signup

MORE SCIENCE FICTION
FROM WORLD WEAVER PRESS

CAMPAIGN 2100: GAME OF SCORPIONS
Larry Hodges

The year is 2100, and the world has adopted the American two-party electoral system. When it comes to the election for president of Earth, the father-daughter team of Toby and Lara Platt are the cutthroat campaign directors who get candidates elected by any means necessary—including the current president, Corbin Dubois of France. But when an alien lands outside the United Nations, claiming to be an ambassador from Tau Ceti, Dubois orders her attacked. Toby resigns.

The alien survives—and so, it seems, might Dubois's corrupt reelection campaign, now run by Lara. But Toby vows to put his daughter out of a job. He challenges the two major parties—one conservative, one liberal—and runs for president himself with a third-party moderate challenge. He's a long-shot, but he's determined to fix the problems he created in getting Dubois elected.

Amid rising tensions and chants of "Alien go home!" the campaign crisscrosses every continent as father and daughter battle for electoral votes and clash over the ideas and issues facing the world of 2100 in this bare-knuckle, fight-to-the-finish political campaign. The world is watching. And so is the alien.

"Larry Hodges is an insightful political commentator and a kick-ass science-fiction writer. A dynamite novel full of twists and turns; this futuristic *House of Cards* is both entertaining and thought-provoking."
—Robert J. Sawyer, Hugo and Nebula Award-winning author of *Quantum Night*

FAR ORBIT
SPECULATIVE SPACE ADVENTURES
Edited by Bascomb James

Featuring stories by award winners **Gregory Benford, Tracy Canfield, Eric Choi, David Wesley Hill**, and more, with an open letter to speculative fiction by **Elizabeth Bear**.

"Put aside all of your preconceived notions of what 'sci-fi' is—whether you think you love it or hate, it doesn't matter—pick up this book and get to reading!"

— Good Choice Reading

FAR ORBIT APOGEE
More modern space adventures
Edited by Bascomb James

Far Orbit Apogee takes all of the fun-to-read adventure, ingenuity, and heroism of mid-century pulp fiction and reshapes it into modern space adventures crafted by a new generation of writers. Follow the adventures of heroic scientists, lunar detectives, space dragons, robots, interstellar pirates, gun slingers, and other memorable and diverse characters as they wrestle with adversity beyond the borders of our small blue marble.

Featuring stories from Jennnifer Campbell-Hicks, Dave Creek, Eric Del Carlo, Dominic Dulley, Nestor Delfino, Milo James Fowler, Julie Frost, Sam S. Kepfield, Keven R. Pittsinger, Wendy Sparrow, Anna Salonen, James Van Pelt, and Jay Werkheiser.

MURDER IN THE GENERATIVE KITCHEN
Meg Pontecorvo

With the Vacation Jury Duty system, jurors can lounge on a comfortable beach while watching the trial via virtual reality. Julio is loving the beach, as well as the views of a curvy fellow juror with a rainbow-lacquered skin modification who seems to be the exact opposite of his recent ex-girlfriend back in Chicago. Because of jury sequestration rules, they can't talk to each other at all, or else they'll have to pay full price for this Acapulco vacation. Still, Julio is desperate to catch her attention. But while he struts and tries to catch her eye, he also becomes fascinated by the trial at hand.

At first it seemed a foregone conclusion that the woman on trial used a high-tech generative kitchen to feed her husband a poisonous meal, but the more evidence mounts, the more Julio starts to suspect the kitchen may have made the decision on its own.

"Mysteriously delicious. Tastefully romantic. With a GMO garnish."
—Terry Bisson, author of *Bears Discover Fire and Other Stories*

"*Murder in the Generative Kitchen* by Meg Pontecorvo is a compact little story with a lot to say. Readers will find a fresh take on Asimov's three laws, see a twisted future where vacations are paid for by the courts, and learn that the same old arguments will still be contested long after we're gone."
—Ricky L. Brown, *Amazing Stories*

"With Murder in the Generative Kitchen, new author Meg Pontecorvo cooks up and dishes out for you not one, not two, but three original sci fi premises. Enjoy and digest them well!"
—David Brin, author of *Existence* and *The Postman*

Sirens

Rhonda Parrish's Magical Menageries, Volume Four

Sirens are beautiful, dangerous, and musical, whether they come from the sea or the sky. Greek sirens were described as part-bird, part-woman, and Roman sirens more like mermaids, but both had a voice that could captivate and destroy the strongest man. The pages of this book contain the stories of the Sirens of old, but also allow for modern re-imaginings, plucking the sirens out of their natural elements and placing them at a high school football game, or in wartime London, or even into outer space.

Featuring stories by Kelly Sandoval, Amanda Kespohl, L.S. Johnson, Pat Flewwelling, Gabriel F. Cuellar, Randall G. Arnold, Michael Leonberger, V. F. LeSann, Tamsin Showbrook, Simon Kewin, Cat McDonald, Sandra Wickham, K.T. Ivanrest, Adam L. Bealby, Eliza Chan, and Tabitha Lord, these siren songs will both exemplify and defy your expectations.

SPECULATIVE STORY BITES

Edited by Sarena Ulibarri

Fifteen bite-sized stories, offering a sampler platter of fantasy, science fiction, and paranormal horror. Within these pages, you'll find flower fairies, alien brothels, were-bears, and sentient houses. Step inside a museum where all the displays are haunted, follow a siren into the underworld as she searches for Persephone, and discover the doors that lie, literally, behind the heart.

Featuring stories by Shannon Phillips, Adam Gaylord, Rebecca Roland, Dianne Williams, M.T. Reiten, Larry Hodges, Anya J. Davis, Jamie Lackey, Megan Neumann, Kristina Wojtaszek, Gregory Scheckler, Sandi Leibowitz, Nora Mulligan, Tom Howard, and A.E. Decker.

World Weaver Press, LLC
Publishing fantasy, paranormal, and science fiction.
We believe in great storytelling.
WorldWeaverPress.com

Made in the USA
Middletown, DE
18 September 2018